THE
COUNTRY
OF
MARRIAGE

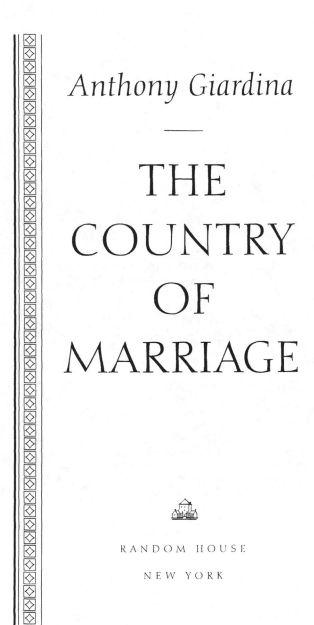

Anthony Giardina

—

THE
COUNTRY
OF
MARRIAGE

RANDOM HOUSE

NEW YORK

Each of the stories in this book is a work of fiction. All incidents and dialogue, and all characters with the exception of a few well-known historical figures, are products of the author's imagination and are not to be construed as real. Any resemblance to persons living or dead is entirely coincidental and unintentional. Where real-life historical figures appear, the situations, incidents, and dialogues concerning those persons are entirely fictional and are not intended to depict any actual events or to change the entirely fictional nature of the work.

Copyright © 1997 by Anthony Giardina

All rights reserved under International and Pan-American Copyright Conventions. Published in the United States by Random House, Inc., New York, and simultaneously in Canada by Random House of Canada Limited, Toronto.

The following stories appeared in slightly different form in these publications: "I Live in Yonville," "Days with Cecilia," "The Cut of His Jib," and "The Lake" in *Harper's*; "The Second Act" in *Esquire*; and "Love, Your Parents" and "The Films of Richard Egan" in *GQ*.

Library of Congress Cataloging-in-Publication Data
Giardina, Anthony.
The country of marriage / Anthony Giardina.
p. cm.
ISBN 978-0-812-99235-9
1. United States—Social life and customs—20th century—Fiction.
2. Married people—United States—Fiction. 3. Marriage—United States—Fiction. 4. Husbands—United States—Fiction. 5. Men—United States—Fiction. I. Title.
PS3557.I135I5 1997
813'.54—dc21   96-40446

Book design by Victoria Wong

146484122

For Nicola and Sophia

ACKNOWLEDGMENTS

Thanks to Laurie Binney, George Gilmore, Wesley Wright and Stephen Cook of the Austin, Texas, Fire Department, the Lyman Street writers—Joann Kobin, Norman Kotker, Mordecai Gerstein, Betsy Hartman, John Stifler, and especially Marisa Labozzetta—Colin Harrison, Valerie Martin, Michael Pettit, Robert Hill Long, Jim Magnuson, Wendy Weil, Deb Futter, and special gratitude to Sloan Harris.

And, as always, Eileen.

CONTENTS

THE
COUNTRY
OF
MARRIAGE

I LIVE
IN YONVILLE

This is going to be a story about marriage. I don't
know any others. It's twelve years for me this
October, and in that time I can't think of much
else that's happened. In the old nineteenth-
century tales, the events of the world somehow
managed to creep into the domestic cottage; bankers came chasing Balzac's bridegrooms, shouting
and pulling out their hair at the fall of the Paris
bank rates. But the world hasn't affected us much.
We bought a house ten years ago, when the rates
were 18 percent. Still, houses were a lot cheaper
then. When the rates went down, we refinanced.

I am a reader, so I can tell you that Flaubert
knew best when he began the story of Emma
Bovary with Charles's school days. Once you
know what an idiot Charles was as a boy, you
understand much better how she is able to fool

him, and why he puts up with her even when he ought to know better. I'm not going to tell you about infidelity here, because as far as I know there isn't any to tell about. But our world is small and provincial like the Bovarys', and if there were secrets here I would probably be the last to know.

As I write this, I am alone. It is that hour of the morning I have to myself. My wife leaves the house at 8:15. She is a medical technician at a hospital twenty miles north of here. My daughter is supposed to leave the house at the same time, but she is a dawdler. She takes her time tying her shoes. I like to have a good bowel movement after the both of them leave; it is the only time I am really fully relaxed. Then I sit at the kitchen table and drink a last cup of coffee and smoke a couple of cigarettes. Two's my limit, usually. I am not due at the office until 9:30.

I mentioned Flaubert before, and that was no idle name-dropping. I barely finished college, but I have kept up. Other men my age, if they read at all, read books by people like Ken Follett and Tom Clancy, while I have been known to come home from the library with a thick copy of *Middlemarch* under my arm. In towns like ours, we use the library. We feel civic-minded and virtuous doing so. It's also a way of saving money, though few besides me will admit it.

As for Flaubert, I am always impressed by the way he has of rooting his stories in the physical space his characters inhabit. Once I was at a party where I didn't know too many people, and some guy came up to me and asked me where I lived. I answered, "I live in Yonville." It was a way of testing how smart he was and also of telling the truth. He didn't get it, but I was proud of myself nonetheless. You can learn a lot about people from just a couple of details like that. I like to know the car a man drives, and how far he has to commute to work. People become dreamy in cars if they have to drive a long way. We put up a great fight against dreaminess by means of car stereos, but I find it's nearly always a losing battle. If I'm talking to someone who has to drive a long way to and from work, I tend to be kinder toward him. I think of this guy surrounded by mountains and fields and the long roads, and I know how you can't help feeling about your life on those long drives. Something creeps into the car with you; it's like the seat beside you doesn't really want to remain empty.

I drive twelve miles to work and twelve back. In the morning there's classical music and in the late afternoon a posh news show in which reporters from the BBC are forever heard shouting over gunfire in places like Baghdad and the West Bank. Last week there was an uprising in Azerbaijan and, sure enough, the BBC was there, shouting. Personally, I couldn't care less what is going on in Azerbaijan, and I don't know anyone who really does. But there seems to be some agreement that at five o'clock, as we all drive home in our cars, we're going to listen to these reports with the attention we reserve for things that matter to us.

The fact is, our world has gotten smaller and smaller, and we've stopped complaining. What's to complain about? I am involved in the local PTO. My wife sends packages of clothes to poor Native American children somewhere in the Southwest. We vote. We cast our nets in the shallows. I write grant proposals for an expensive women's college. Our friends are doctors, tradesmen, local professionals. We are proud of our little world. Though no one would come out and say this outright, we consider ours a model for the way all towns should be. We vote Democratic and don't object too strenuously to a rise in taxes. We think of our children as enlightened.

I know some people who are unmarried, but not many.

That fact—along with all the preceding information—might make it sound like my life is totally homogenized, but I don't consider it so. I find great variety in the country of marriage. Always, you have to interpret the world through the subtlest of clues. We are forced to become detectives of each other, a far more interesting proposal, to my mind, than the naked emotionalism of the unattached. Divorce drops like sudden death among us. All the clues were there, but none of us picked up on them, so we have something to discuss for weeks. Who needs to listen to the news when we have the spectacle of Roberta Hawkins, who used to stay home baking tomato cakes for her husband, hitting the bars and bringing around a new boyfriend every week? The BBC would never think of coming here, and that is why we smile—I smile—when we hear the announcer's voice. It's as though he's stuck in an old version of the world. Or perhaps—who knows?—I am.

It's hard to remember exactly, but it seems five or six years ago I stopped thinking beyond my immediate circle. Before then, I suppose I was ambitious. I got this job, at least, which pays me well, though I don't see any real chance that I'll rise. Some other person might want to tell you this story from the inside out, but not me. I look around myself and there I see my story. When I'm alone for even a night away from here, I panic. This house and the car and the job, and, of course, the marriage, are what I've become. I'm not complaining.

Maybe you're a curious person and you want to know what I look like. Let's just say I'm one of those people you see on the beach in summer—we go to Wellfleet, ourselves—and don't wonder too much about. I'm small and slightly built, and my hair won't grow. It's always short.

When it does grow, it grows unevenly no matter how it's cut, so I don't fight it, I just keep it short. I've been told I'm not bad-looking, but I don't have what I suppose you'd call a sexual presence. I'm one of those men who might as well be women.

We recognize one another, I think, and make our friendships accordingly. There are certain men I just don't know what to say to. They seem to be savages to me, different entirely. I don't know what they want. You know the sort of men I'm talking about. Maybe you're one of them. If so, write the story of your life please, because I'd like to know it. When I pick up a contemporary novel that promises to lay bare what the cover describes as "the macho heart," I am generally disappointed. I am convinced there are more differences between us than the novelists allow. These "macho heart" novels are most likely written by men like me, men who are only guessing.

My friends are all as soft as marshmallows. We joke about one another's bellies, but no one really cares. None of us plays competitive sports, though we swim and run. We are the ones who failed at high school athletics. We are the ones the girls never liked. We consider ourselves lucky—blessed, even—because we found a girl to like us. We're not the ones you're going to catch sleeping with other women. Sometimes when we're alone in bars (it's rare) we marvel at the fact that all around us men are cheating on their wives. We stare at one another and laugh and ask: Who? It's the same game the virgins used to play in high school. There's a raw world and there's a tame one, and I believe you make the choice early as to which you're going to live in.

✉

I'm on my third cigarette now. I know I shouldn't smoke, but I do. Everyone needs a vice. I don't even masturbate anymore. I think cigarettes prolong time, so I smoke them and look out the window and consider things. Then I get in the car, where the classical-music station is already deeply into Dvořák or Schumann. I cross the mountains some mornings in a state approaching what I remember it felt like to meditate. If you've been here, you know what the light is like. I'm proud to drive a good car, a Volkswagen Scirocco. I bought it new, three years ago.

At work, I joke with the girls. There are two of them. I'm the only man. Sheri does clerical work. Elaine works with me. She's from New York, married and divorced, looking. We eat lunch together. She discusses datelessness and I sympathize. She tells me I'm easy to talk to.

There are moments of the day that are difficult, of course. What day doesn't contain its emptinesses? For me, these moments usually arrive in the afternoon, after lunch, when the light begins to change. The fact is, I don't like the afternoon light here. It has the quality of seeming damp and harsh at once. It's a light like the emptying out of drawers. I am one of those men for whom the most sensual exercise of the day is the imagination of dinner. But at around three P.M. a dismal kind of fear starts up in me. I lose the thread of things. Usually I get a cup of coffee. It's the moment when I know that if I make a call, the person I am calling will not be there.

When our daughter was little, my fear always used to center on her. The day had a built-in drama, since it was never a given that the two of them, mother and child, would make it through the day unscathed. We had only one car then; they would drive me to work in the morning. At my desk, I would practically count the minutes until I could call them, in order to assure myself that they'd negotiated the passage safely. This was especially intense in winter, when there was ice on the roads.

Those days are over. I have ceased worrying for their safety. Something else troubles me now. It makes its appearance always in the form of an ambush. Sometimes it disappears quickly; still, it leaves me unsettled for the day.

Charles Bovary, had he been as bright as I am, would have recognized this feeling, since it was all around him. All he had to do was look up from his medical books. Perhaps he was wise not to. It is nothing so small as adultery, which seems to me now a forgivable thing. He was one with the life of Yonville. He saw nothing he couldn't excuse. But I see, at those moments of the day when the unwelcome light slants through the windows of the Grant Proposal Office, that few of us get away with this life we pretend to be living. Once maybe, but not anymore. On the green lawn of the Unitarian church each week a new inspirational slogan goes up on the announcement board. The quotes are secular, from writers and scientists and thinkers. This week it's "Blessed are the dreamers, for some of their dreams will come true." I forget the author. On Sundays we all smile and nod at one another, as if these are the things we truly believe, these are the truths that will see us through.

My problem, of course, is that I don't believe them. It takes a certain kind of light to force me to acknowledge this. On the drive home, I pass the Unitarian church and wonder for a moment what it would be like to deface the announcement board, or replace it with something like: "We've all been lucky so far, that's all."

⊠

At night, the three of us gather around the table and eat what is usually a good dinner. My wife works hard all day, but she manages to find the energy to cook us something original every night. Stir-fried pork and cauliflower, that sort of thing. White pizza with ricotta cheese. She's a beautiful woman, and our daughter is inheriting the shape of her face, her chin and eyes. We've talked about having another child. To tell you the truth, neither of us could probably say why we haven't done it. Sometimes I think it's necessary to see a thing before you can make it happen—we talk about this a lot in the fund-raising business—and I guess we just don't see ourselves as the sort of big jovial family so many people pretend to want. We think we're fine as three. We like our silences, our times alone. We worry about loneliness—our daughter's in particular—but when things are weighed in the balance, we end up doing nothing to change our lot. I suppose I harbor some jealousy against people with large families, but I don't want to be them.

After our daughter goes to sleep, my wife and I have the nights to ourselves. She watches television, and I read. I feel guilty about her having to spend her days with blood and shit and urine; part of me feels I've been deficient in romance, or that I haven't supported her in any of her more ambitious endeavors. She once wanted to be a dancer. The more I talk to people, the more I realize everyone's wife once wanted to be a dancer. Now all these good women are nurses and teachers and therapists, and no one complains. We talk about our romantic youths, but mine was never romantic, and the fear I have is that I've taken some part of my terror of the world and planted it in her. So I write grant proposals all day, and she studies people's evacuations for signs of disease. We have our responsible lives, and at night we stay quietly at home, two good citizens in our little town.

It's only after my wife goes to bed that I start drinking. The day has its fault lines and this is one of them. I can't go to sleep early, but those hours alone in a house with two sleeping women are hard for me. It's like the fear that started up with the afternoon change in light returning in force. Nothing else can assuage it, not TV, not the book I happen to be reading. I drink a little scotch, a little ice, and I wait for sleep.

I remember the night—this was before I started drinking—when I read Turgenev's "First Love." I don't know if you've read it, but there's a passage at the end to break your heart. The young hero grows up and discovers that the beautiful Zinaida, his first love, the girl he jumped from the roof of the greenhouse for, has died. But it is not her death he mourns at the end. Instead, he remembers the death of an old servant who had nothing to live for, but who, in dying, grasps at the remains of life as if her miserable existence had suddenly appeared to her as the most precious, extraordinary thing. The night I read that I started crying. I went into my daughter's room and looked at her face and cried some more. Then I went and sat and watched my wife sleeping, and it was all too much. I thought that night that I was at the very center of my life, as if I'd slid down a long sloping wall that had landed me in this moment and I was facing that wall's opposite, one that instead of sliding down I would have to climb. For all I know, that's when it began. I vowed that night to be good. It was one of those moments.

But I've found that such vows don't amount to much. There's a kind of knowledge that undoes you. Partly, it's knowing that fate has done its share of the work, has landed you where it's landed you, but that after a certain point it's not fate anymore but the particular direction one places one's feet that makes all the difference in the world. For a while you're sliding but then you're walking, and if there's a way to walk and not watch yourself at the same time I don't know it. The feeling of that night, anyway, has numbed over. It's what happens, I guess. My vow was that I would stay and watch them both die, if I had to. But since then I've become too aware, in these moments of solitude, that other choices are available to me. Sometimes, driving home from work in a light that threatens to suffocate, I become aware of the fact that I could continue driving, just go somewhere else and begin all over again. I imagine making a collect call home from a phone in Ohio, or Indiana. What's frightening is the way this imagined moment has a certain ghostly ring to it, like it's already happened.

That would be the clean break, of course. Instead, I'm fooling no one. I smoke these cigarettes, I drink this scotch. I do these things in moderation, but is anyone these days fooled by moderation? I am a timid soul, and I do nothing to excess. I couldn't smoke a pack of cigarettes a day if I tried. I'd puke. And I'd puke if I drank more than three glasses of scotch a night. I wouldn't know how to explain any of this to my wife. She counts on me for the sort of steady, sober behavior that gives our life together stability. She doesn't know I smoke, and the scotch glass, if I neglect to wash it at night before I go to bed, she makes excuses for. Bourgeois males are supposed to drink at night. That's how the thinking goes.

After a point there's really not much sense to locking the door at night. Whatever terrors are out there seem nothing.

My brother-in-law tells me about a friend of his, a good husband, an accountant, who feels compelled some nights to get into his Le Mans and drive from Westchester into Harlem. He picks up whores. He throws caution to the wind. A while ago I heard about a guy from around here whose wife was eight and a half months pregnant. Out of the blue, he took a trip to the Himalayas to climb the highest, slipperiest mountain there. In spite of my timid soul, I feel I understand these actions, as I pour my third scotch of the night or light up my fourth cigarette. There is always the hope, the off chance, that life will prove too much for us and we'll get out of this thing with some grace. It is the nature of terror that it not have a distinct visage, and that it not announce itself in daylight hours on the face of its prey, and so you will wonder, as you pass me, or other men like me, in the autumn, and catch a glimpse of us raking our lawns, our sons and daughters at play around us, how such a desirable life can contain such an appetite for its own destruction. But I assure you it's there, for those few of us who are like Emma, who simply cannot sit comfortably in these lives anymore without conjuring a beast staring squarely at us, measuring us and holding out almost tentatively, if beasts can be said to be tentative, the vial of M. Homais's arsenic.

You will, of course, dismiss this, say I'm being melodramatic, and to a degree you will be right. The feeling comes and goes, and there's no predicting its approach or its duration. For the most part, I am a happy man.

It's clear by now I'm going to be late this morning. Not that it matters. There are no appointments on my calendar until Thursday. Until then, I'm just filling time.

I crush my fourth cigarette, but something won't let me

head for the door, not yet. This is a good kitchen. We worked hard putting it together, and the method of food preparation here is serious. I like nothing better than to watch my wife cook. On Saturday nights, when we put our daughter to bed early, I pour myself a glass of wine and watch her do something fancy, an orange sauce or chicken mole. At such moments I feel as far from the terror as I ever do. The warmth in the room is tangible, and I can say whatever I want to say. Something will uphold us, suspend us in its net. I haven't told you much about my wife, but I don't want you to get the impression that there isn't a lot to tell. She is stubborn, she is mostly her own woman, and she loves me. There is the sort of intimacy between us that is the reason everyone stays married, and there is the nakedness and shame that makes everyone want to bolt. To tell the story of a marriage, I think you only need to tell one side. In learning about me, you can conjure my opposite, and I'd venture to guess you won't be far off. I never am, at least, when I meet a spouse after getting to know her groom a little bit. You get to know their terrors and their desires, and after a while you come to understand there's only one sort of person who could hold those particular demons at bay. So if you need to imagine my wife, think of that woman you see on the beach sometimes, more beautiful than her husband deserves. To yourself, you think: They married young.

Still, they stay married, so something must be there. Whatever it is, it makes its appearance over our good expensive counter on those Saturday nights, and the reason I can't quite leave this kitchen now is the chance that some part of it might still be in the air, like an old scent the oven fan can't get rid of. We cut a hole out of the air for ourselves. It's no more than that, really, and the reason it doesn't survive is: What is there in the world to support bubbles? That's all that marriages are, really: bubbles. But while they float in the air, they have an enormous attractiveness. If I put this cigarette out and head for the door, it's only because I want to get to the next Saturday night.

I'm on my fifth cigarette now, but I can feel the danger's past. I'm going to go and see Sheri and Elaine and think about how we can shake the Mellon Foundation for a few extra thou. I can feel the energy for this, though I have no idea where it's coming from, just as, later, I will have no idea where it went. At the end of the day, I'll listen to the fighting in provinces of the Soviet Union, the BBC, and I'll try to pay attention, try to place my moments of panic beside my moments of calm, to convince myself that life contains a balance. There will be moments—I can be assured of this—when I'll want to send up a wild howl. But I'll stifle that urge. Light always changes, I'll remind myself. It only stays hard for a while.

It seems to me that life requires us, as time goes on, to become masters of convincing ourselves of the simplest things. To prefer life to death, for one. I have this twelve-mile ride ahead of me this morning. I have Dvořák for consolation, and there are these dips at the side of the road it would be so easy to go over. On Saturday nights, my wife cooks wonderful chicken things. I'll try to remember that.

There. I've put it out. I suppose that means something. Barely smoked. Live or die. They say maturity is not caring so much. I wouldn't know. I have a photograph of my wife I keep in the glove compartment of the car. It helps, I find sometimes, to take it out and look at it out of the corner of my eye as I drive. It's a simple picture, really, taken outside a beach house we rented once. It was a cloudy Sunday. Perhaps you know the way the clouds look on a late summer afternoon on the Cape. She had developed a sty that day, and was wearing sunglasses. In the photograph, she sits on a weathered wooden chair, staring directly into the camera. Her eyes are hidden, but the expression is unmistakable. It's nothing you can put into words. She is a woman in a chair on a late summer afternoon, that's all. Still, I can't look at it without thinking she is asking me to come closer. And in my imagination—at least on days like this, when one thing seems better than another—I do.

DAYS WITH CECILIA

My days with Cecilia are crowded with the props
of the slim British novels my wife devours. Half-
eaten slices of cold toast, semi-warm tea with the
pale milk scud lying discouragingly on top; that
sort of thing. I often parade around in ratty underwear, and when Cecilia sleeps I can most often
be found combing the police log of already-read
metropolitan newspapers for the details of grisly
murders. It goes without saying I am perpetually
behind things. I enjoy a strange identification with
the spinster librarians in those books of my wife's,
those perpetually hopeful overage girls who live in
a fog out of which they can't quite penetrate to the
fact of the balding pediatrician's less than honest
intentions. But in most ways we are not alike. My
life, as I prefer to view it, is full of facts, closely
looked at.

I'd like to say, for instance, that Cecilia is bright, or exceptionally precocious. The fact is, I wouldn't know how to compare her with the average child; we don't see any. Occasionally we pass them in the park, but though Cecilia's head always perks up in these instances, as though she'd like nothing better than to rub noses with another ten-month-old, I don't think I could bear to get involved in one of those conversations I occasionally overhear between parents on park benches. They have nothing whatsoever in common outside of the base facts of parenthood, so what gets talked about is Justin's progress with the walker, Julie's teething habits and extraordinary verbal facility, and the problems poor Mrs. L—— is having with her son, who at sixteen months has yet to take his first step. Let's not fool ourselves—beneath this seemingly casual comparison of achievement lies the most savage competition, a clawing for the superiority of one's own over another's barely masked. To hell with Justin and Julie, I say; Cecilia and I push on.

She is a happy child; I think I can say that without too crippling a sense of doubt. She likes nothing better than to grasp the edge of an end table with one hand and lift herself so that she's standing unsupported (can you do *that*, Justin and Julie?) and, in recognition of the feat, crow with delight. At such moments, I am superfluous. I am the man on the couch in ratty underwear, trying not to catch furtive glimpses of himself in whatever mirror happens to be lurking nearby. I am her caretaker; I clock the hours between waking and sleeping, with time out for naps. My wife doesn't come home until after she's asleep most days; I know why, and I don't care to comment. There is a ruddy and obnoxious economist she's taken up with, a fellow member of her department at the university. A mutual friend informed me, expecting I'd do something about it, but I haven't, and suspect I won't.

By trade I am a shop teacher, part-time. My employer is a very expensive private middle school two towns away. It sits on the side of a hill on land donated by one of those families—you know the ones I mean—whose name conjures an aura of sacrosanct white privilege, but whom I cannot imagine without the accompanying vision of pristine white body parts squatting atop porcelain chamber pots. Perhaps this image is a result of the fact that Cecilia shits so much, but I like to believe that my mind is not so cause-and-effect. The red buildings of the grounds are ancient brick and smell of the exertions of generations. The place is athletic as all hell and justifiably proud of its many trophies. In a room that might have served the lathers of the eighteenth century, I train the boys to shave a block of wood straight, smooth, and square. For the satisfactory performance of this job, I am required only two afternoons a week. Shop is not a high priority at the Russell Academy.

That I happen to be doing this job: well, we're all old enough not to require explanations anymore, or to believe them when they're offered. My own shop teacher from twenty years past was Mr. Chilingerian, an Armenian rumored to have thrown a hammer from twenty feet at a wisecracking boy. Like my classmates of those days, I saw little beyond the truism that shop teachers are brutes. Either that or something less. So my boys—my Barneses and Neuwirths and Hulls—view me, I'm sure, in an opaque light. I am dim and incomprehensible in my soiled blue shop coat. The lights are caged and ancient, of a piece with Russell. Once a boy nearly took a finger off learning to use the electric saw. I saved him in the nick of time and watched how, five minutes later, laughing, he had managed to forget both the saved finger and my quick heroism—a necessary part of the job, as I see it—and would most likely soon be back to making fun of me behind my back. No matter.

On Tuesdays and Thursdays, when I am at work, Cecilia stays with Mrs. Leaver, who charges me four dollars an hour for the service. It is a decent arrangement, and loose enough so that, after the last of the boys have left the shop for the day, I am free to linger, in the shop or on the grounds, enjoying the fading light and the last moments of relaxed freedom before going to pick up Cecilia. It is at such moments, as the low light slides in under the blinds onto the clean shop table or as I stand at the edge of the playing fields, that I allow myself my one moment of fantastic longing: for a friend like those friends one encounters in films, a short, thick-bellied, wide-faced man with a name like Colin or George, either married or in constant woman trouble, but not bothered much by either state of affairs, a fellow shop or perhaps mathematics teacher, who, at the end of the day, is always available and eager for a hop down to the pub (in my imagination there is one at the foot of the Russell grounds), where we might sit and chat about things like football scores, all the while engaging in our true business, which is what I will call a muscular and disciplined appreciation of the qualities of light and silence.

Such a moment—altogether male as I see it, but I'm willing to be convinced otherwise—is the one thing lacking in my days. No such friend exists. Colin is an invention of the film writers. We are all busy, and have to plan even the briefest, least satisfactory of encounters weeks in advance. There is no pub at the foot of the hill. The long playing fields stretch out these days in shades of ocher and sienna, but as I stand at the edge of them I am only too keenly aware that Mrs. Leaver has been expecting me for fifteen minutes already, and Cecilia can't be ignored much longer.

So I hop in the car and drive the quarter mile to the two-family house where Mrs. Leaver lives with her two children in what I perceive to be a state of happy squalor. At least, she is always laughing as she clears away the line of tricycles and children's toys that block her path to the door. I stand there, watching through the lace curtain that hangs on the other side of the glass, noticing the too-tight pants, the half inch or so of exposed midriff as Mrs. Leaver bends to move a Fisher-Price Activity Center. There is no Mr. Leaver, apparently; at some indeterminate time in the past, he headed for the hills. On the faces of the two Leaver children, a boy and a girl, barely school age, I detect the droop-jawed neediness of the abandoned. They are angry children, given to kicking walls on what seem to be the slightest of pretexts.

Mrs. Leaver notices none of this, of course, and screams at them to stop kicking, meanwhile turning back to me with a broad smile to share a joke or to ask after my adventures in the Russell shop. Cecilia clings to me as soon as she is handed over, and I feel a certain guilt at splitting my attention in order to afford some to Mrs. Leaver, who seems to relish a bit of adult companionship at this point in the day. Certain looks and gestures have led me to believe Mrs. Leaver would like nothing better than for me to make a pass, if only for the opportunity of shrugging it off, or both of us raising our eyes to heaven as if to say, "If only it weren't for these children, what larks!" In fact, what I am thinking at such moments is that it is *only* the children who are keeping us from the unbearable chaos of a shag in the half-abandoned Leaver bed. I see the two of us groping and kicking there and I want to grab Cecilia and dash for the safety of the house.

There are only the two of us in the station wagon on the ride home, myself behind the wheel, Cecilia in the plastic car seat, and it does seem at those moments as though we are negotiating a kind of minefield, while Cecilia hums one of those secret melodies which signify to me that, for her, the minefield is limited to Mrs. Leaver's rooms and halls.

There was a woman before Mrs. Leaver. Mrs. O'Connor. She disapproved of us. Babies belonged with their mothers. That the world had seen fit to discard this truth constituted the basis of Mrs. O'Connor's argument with the universe, and the argument had settled like a pall over the modest day-care business the woman conducted from her home. "Poor baby," she would croon, as soon as I handed Cecilia over to her, and I stood racked with guilt for the hours afterward, as I attempted to explain the principle of going with the grain to Barnes, Neuwirth, and Hull. "She barely ate, poor thing," Mrs. O'Connor would tut when handing the baby over, and in that tut was contained something akin to the moral furor of the Nuremberg judges.

The cruel truth is that perhaps men don't, after all, belong with babies. I've thought this myself, wondered why, if the idea were such a good one, we seem to be the first people in history to have thought of it. And lest you come back with a counter-argument too quickly, let me remind you that we are also the first people in history to have come up with aerosol cans and magazines with titles like *Self.* The rigors of advanced capitalism force us into odd and twisted postures, and this notion of men as nurturers may be just another one of them. I was recently in a diner in some nearby town, feeding Cecilia her favorite lunch of mashed banana and Cheerios, when the local execs started trooping in. One man in particular was noticeable. He could not get a knife clean enough, kept sending them back. Then he started on the forks. There was a pronounced tic in the man's facial gesture as he sent back utensil after utensil, a kind of astonished blinking. And as I mused on what horrors of unnatural activity had forced him into such neurotic behavior, I noticed myself mashing bananas and Cheerios together with a pronounced rhythm that might, from his table, have looked at least equally strange. The only reason I hesitate to carry this argument further is that I might find myself agreeing with Mrs. O'Connor, and no thanks, I'd rather not.

One night last week my wife came home at her usual time—nine o'clock—and headed straight for the bath, her usual practice. I generally have something simmering on the stove when she gets home—this particular night I had cooked pork chops in olive oil and rosemary, with a roasted pepper dressing—but I make sure it is something that will keep and not dry out during the ritual bath taking. I don't want you to think that she is one of those women—or ours one of those marriages—constructed of cold silences and an ironclad respect for the Unsaid, though on the surface that might be what appears. I think of it as a peculiarly *living* thing, and for that reason don't need to bother her as to the lateness of the hour or the lack of interest she displays in Cecilia's welfare. By this time, Cecilia is snug and in her crib, wrapped in a double diaper and a woolen yellow sleeper. In her bath, my wife washes out what there is to be washed out of her, the leavings of the economist Bruce

Friedman. I could ask after him, and after a pause and a considering lift of the eyebrows, I'm sure my wife would tell me everything, without tears or mortification. I like that aspect of things, and for that reason have never felt compelled to ask. I waited this night outside the bathroom until she'd done what she had to do and then stepped in.

The bath is not quite full-length; it's a bit cramped, if the truth be told, so a body lying full-length looks somewhat less resplendent than it ought to. My wife's breasts have long since returned to their pre-pregnancy shape (she quit nursing at three weeks), but her middle retains a pleasing lumpen aspect, the last of Cecilia's nesting. She's a good-looking woman whose body, unfortunately, leaves me cold. Has since the day she brought Cecilia home. Hence, Bruce. So we can leave that subject and move on. But this one night I sat on the toilet and stared at her and waited for her to acknowledge me. She was soaping her breasts at the time. I was wearing a blue bathrobe that had seen better days. (Get on with it! you charge at this juncture. Fix yourself up and perhaps your life's problems will be solved!)

"How did it go?" I asked.

"Department meeting," she answered, still not looking up. "The usual shit."

"Did you eat lunch?" I asked, in my mothering tone.

She told me what she'd eaten, and then some departmental gossip. For her, there is still the illusion to be maintained that these late evenings are caused by work. I helped dry her off, a process I enjoy, in large part I think because it reminds me of drying Cecilia. Then she ate the pork chops and drank the wine I'd poured her, and the two of us took out the foldout couch and lay there watching a Michael Caine spy movie from the sixties. It was of the genre where the filmmakers tried very hard to distinguish their man from James Bond, with thick glasses and such. I believe they called this at the time a Greater Realism. In other words, there was absolutely nothing unusual about this night except what happened midway through the spy picture. My bathrobe happened to be open, unintentionally, and at the point where Michael Caine was about to be tortured my wife reached over and lifted my penis. It is quite a long one (or so I've been told), and as she held it there, limp but extended upward by her grasp, it bisected the image of Michael Caine's grimacing face. She held it for the length of time it took for the torture to be completed and then put it back in place. A commercial came on and we lay there in a kind of awed silence. As soon as the movie came back on, I began reporting on Cecilia's day, my concern about an incipient ear infection. My wife listened, quite patient and interested, but not as though this information being imparted was anything she was going to have to act on. In a short while, before the movie was finished, she fell asleep, then roused herself and went upstairs to bed. I stayed up awhile. I checked on Cecilia. It was early spring but it had snowed during the night and outside our windows I could see it falling. I was trying to connect things, and having a hard time of it. In my mind was the image of Bruce Friedman thrashing away between my wife's thighs in a manner I imagined as resembling the behavior of a crazed member of the college crew team. Then there was the holding of my penis. In her little room at the top of the house my daughter slept, and outside was the snow, gentle and unthreatening and more a reminder that winter was over than that some new and tremendous difficulty lay ahead. I planned my lesson for the next day, and then I, too, got into bed and fell asleep.

◫

Cecilia was up early the next day, so I changed her and fed her a bottle. Then I sat her on her high chair and let her play with some teething things while I fixed my wife her eggs. It seemed to me as I did these things that something was noticeably different. I went through these rituals trying to put my finger on it and failing. Each time I tried to affix this difference to a specific prospect—would my penis finally stand? would my wife stop seeing the economist Friedman?—I found these things to be insignificant and unworthy of the larger pleasure I was experiencing.

I pondered all this while Cecilia gummed her Mr. Happy toy and the yellow eggs bubbled on the grill. My wife was late for her first class and barely had time to gobble the eggs, kiss Cecilia, and dash out the door. I got no kiss. I had a cup of coffee and smoked a cigarette and read the obituary of a man who had been influential in the Eisenhower administration. At ten, Cecilia slept, and at noon I drove her to Mrs. Leaver's and then went myself to the shop, arriving fifteen minutes before my class, a decent interval, and began laying out materials for the day's lesson in soldering.

It went fairly well. Hot metal is quite a pleasant thing to work with, but dangerous, and Barnes, Neuwirth, Hull, and the others never appear so vulnerable as when they first hold the hot soldering iron in their hands and begin moving the liquid metal around. There are moments in the day— this was one of them—when their faces, ravaged as they are by the crocus shoots of incipient puberty, seem to strip back to the point where they appear as babies again, naked and innocent as Cecilia, with powdered bums and fingers like the pincers of crabs. My wife has a friend, a woman from the university, who comes to dinner occasionally. One night we got to talking, in the manner of people who have perhaps spent too much time in college towns, about the nature of reality. "I don't suppose we live it," my wife offered. "People in New York live it. People in the streets." I had nothing to offer on the subject—perhaps if I had it would have been something to do with Michael Caine and the heavy-rimmed glasses he wore in the spy picture—but I remember the woman smirking at the end of my wife's comment. "You're being sentimental," she said. "You know how sometimes in the afternoon, you take a nap, at two or three, and when you wake up it's never the way it is when you wake up in the morning? There are several seconds— they're delicious—when you have no life. The facts have to catch up with you." She picked up her fork and started eating again. "That's reality. The moments before the facts catch up." I remembered that comment as I watched Barnes, Neuwirth, and Hull grapple with the mysteries of soldering. Soon they would be skilled enough to draw erotic figures in hot metal. I have seen them etch enormous phalluses and breasts in wood; it seems to be their primary joy, once they have mastered a skill, to impress one another with the lewd purposes to which it can be put. But they were not yet at this point with soldering; that is, the facts hadn't caught up, and they stood at their places, holding their irons with a kind of wondering detachment.

When the class was over, I went into the teachers' room and had a cup of coffee. I hadn't been inside this room since my first day at Russell, when the headmaster, in the midst of a tour of the facilities, had insisted I step inside and "meet the staff." Two women speaking French in a corner of the room had scared me off that day. I'm almost ashamed to admit this, since by now you will have guessed that I am a sensitive type, but it is no exaggeration to say that these two rare birds showed contempt for me that day. We'd caught them in the middle of a discussion. They were discussing Flaubert's *"Un Coeur Simple,"* as I recall, and did not take to being interrupted. Oh, they were very civil, but when you've been around academics as long as I have—especially low-grade academics, the not-yet-tenured, the private-school types—you begin to sort out the ones who are afraid of you. God knows where this fear comes from—perhaps it's my very shagginess, the air I seem to give off, with my long hair and my soiled blue shop coat, of being a rough guy, that makes them fluff their feathers and nest more defensively over the egg of their pretensions. Or perhaps it is not fear at all, but something else. Whatever, they gave off a skunkish stink that day, and I have kept away ever since. So you can imagine the degree of confidence—the extent of my good mood—as I sauntered into the teachers' room this particular day and sought out the cup with my name on it that had been gathering dust on the shelf for over a year.

I was wearing my blue shop coat still—no shame there—and, well, if you must know, I was hoping to find Colin. It was not until I'd poured the coffee and sat down to drink it that I noticed there was only one other person in the room. A woman sat on the edge of a sofa puffing great blue streams into the air from slender brown cigarettes. She peered at me through this haze, and said, after a point, "You're the shop teacher, aren't you?"

"Yes."

She stared out the window.

"Teaching Thomas Hardy is very difficult," she said.

It was all she said. Her smoking was languid, and highly studied, of a piece with the fold of her legs and the high severe neckline of her dress. I wondered what the proper response was: "Teaching soldering is likewise a bitch"?

Would that have started us off on a stimulating inter-disciplinary chat? I'll never know, because I said nothing. Instead, I began thinking of Mrs. Leaver, who was in any case never far from my mind during these stolen moments after the close of shop. What would Mrs. Leaver have made of such a comment, among her toys and the persistent smell of urine? At the moment, I felt a silent communion with Mrs. Leaver, knew a desire to join up with her, put my hands into the muck of child rearing, to smell the soft wet smell and draw to my nose the small astonished body of Cecilia. There was nothing for me in this room, I understood, and was about to go when a new man entered. Obviously in a hurry, he shouted, "Hello, Peg," quickly poured himself a cup of coffee, and bolted it, standing stiff and upright before the urn, taking it black. He was a thin man, with suede patches on the elbows of his jacket, and the sort of head that seems to make itself over after the age of forty, so that no trace of the youth he might once have enjoyed remained. Once he noticed me, he stood staring for several seconds, rapidly blinking his eyes in the manner of a man trying to wake up quickly, with no time to enjoy the fuzzy-headedness of waking.

Finally, as if something had just occurred to him, he half-shouted, "Shop, is it?"

I nodded, he checked his watch and ran for the door, and that was the end of that.

When I picked up Cecilia that day, I was more than usually solicitous of Mrs. Leaver, which led her to offer me something, a cup of tea or a drink. I declined but Mrs. Leaver went ahead, poured bourbon over ice. Cecilia was more or less content in my arms and we watched Mrs. Leaver drink.

"Your wife teaches, doesn't she?" Mrs. Leaver asked. She

already knew this, and was just making conversation, but I answered that yes, she did, and yes, Cecilia was my responsibility, day in, day out. It must be difficult, she said, and I answered, no, it really isn't. With your wife away all the time, I mean.

Well, here is the juncture where things become problematical, because though I find it difficult to talk to the Pegs and the *coeurs simples* of this world, there are fine distinctions in any life which they might be able to receive with less effort than Mrs. Leaver. You see, I had an answer for Mrs. Leaver but wasn't sure I ought to give it. Was it difficult with my wife away all the time? Well, no. The birth of children brings on a kind of winnowing, as I see it, like the selection of the swim team, where some are going to make it and some are not. Or no, perhaps that's wrong, though the diving metaphor is probably right. We are brought to the edge of a cliff and asked to dive. It's perfectly natural that some will prefer not to. In most cases, though, one of the partners will be willing, and the other left to find some distraction somewhere. The roles get sorted quite satisfactorily, and the only problem comes when, at the end of the day, the two meet and try to proceed as though everything is perfectly rational. What can there possibly be to talk about over the stir-fried chicken when one has been diving off a cliff all day, while the other has been operating a staple gun or conjugating French verbs? That we try to communicate at all is where we run into trouble, and consequently it is all a story of abandonment and betrayal, a fact Mrs. Leaver would readily understand if I could find words simple enough. My wife would like me to make wild love to her every night just to assure her that my day has been like hers. But I find I cannot; the act has become inessential.

Would Mrs. Leaver comprehend any of this if I made the attempt to speak, or is it better to leave it alone, unspoken and therefore brought closer to its true weight in the world? It occurred to me just then that Mrs. Leaver is my Colin, this ratty house of hers our leafy pub. And as I watched her down her bourbon, I thought: yes, all right, it'll do. She's my man, my silent compatriot. I wrapped up Cecilia and drove home.

My wife was there already, a surprise. Her little Volvo sat parked in the driveway like a note left there for me. Inside, she was cooking. It was clear right away she had come home to save her marriage. I imagined somewhere on campus the economist Friedman running hard laps to sweat off the effects of his deprivation. It was angel-hair pasta she was cooking, with zucchini and prosciutto. Lovely. A recipe from the old days, before Cecilia, when my wife still liked to cook.

I kissed her and busied myself with Cecilia. Already I could see I had done something wrong. My wife was pouting as she lay strips of prosciutto on a plate. That she was here, she believed, ought to have altered things more than was presently visible. What I wanted to tell her was that the rhythms of a baby's day are eternal and weather events more climactic than an errant wife's return. As the lifeboats were lowered off the *Titanic*, I imagine all the mothers onboard opening their little jars of baby food; six o'clock is six o'clock, iceberg or no iceberg. I fed Cecilia and felt my wife's presence, and thought of the spurned economist under the shower, the hot gush of water parting his thin hair (mine is marvelously long and thick), sloping over his beard like lather, then down his broad chest and off the spout of his ridiculous genitals. In my mind's eye, the water became hot metal, and there was a soldering gun in my hand, which I used to part his pale, humbled cheeks . . . well, enough of that. I hadn't known I was this jealous, and I'm not sure even now whether it wasn't an effect of the imbalance caused by my wife's sudden appearance. I could smell the butter and cream now. Some sensual promise seemed to hang on the air, but what I ought to do, what action to take, eluded me completely.

During dinner, I was, as usual, solicitous of Cecilia. It's what she's grown used to, after all, my presence at dinner, humming and murmuring shy endearments. These annoy my wife, which is one of the reasons her returning late has never bothered me. She kept refilling my wineglass like an underappreciated husband eager for his wife's attention, and I kept resisting these pleas, turning to Cecilia and making up reasons to fuss. To tell the truth, I was up against one of those black holes, those unexpected places where the lines of one's behavior go underground. If you were to ask me even now why I was resisting my wife, I could offer you any number of explanations, but none of them, I am sure, would be even close to the truth. As far as I could tell, the problem was fairly simple: we wanted different things.

What *I* wanted was to watch the video I had picked up on the way home from Mrs. Leaver's. *The Train*, with Burt Lancaster. Burt plays a French Resistance leader determined to prevent a Nazi train containing hundreds of absconded masterpieces from reaching the German border. Paul Scofield is the Nazi who's got to keep Burt from succeeding. Why I am partial to movies like this is another black hole, but there's no denying it. I had looked forward to getting Cecilia to bed and popping the video into the recorder, then lying back and watching Burt and Paul fight over paintings, using the terse, witless, but perfectly functional dialogue characteristic of the classier sixties films. I would lie there, feeling splendid, wholly absorbed in the action, and my wife would join me after her bath, yawn once or twice and ask me to fill her in on the plot, then fall asleep before the final shoot-out. I'd cover her and fall asleep myself after rewinding the spool. Such evenings, fruitless but oddly satisfying, are the dark heart of any smoothly running domestic existence. The point is to beat slowly. The point is to remain unexcited, to run at a steady pace. This was the wisdom I had attained after years of trial and error. And here was my wife with the dinner and the wine and I knew I might as well forget *The Train*.

When I brought this up, she gave me one of those looks: yet another of your dreary movies, which you watch only to avoid having to deal with me. She was quite certain she could see right through me, and I knew it would serve no purpose to point out that what she was seeing was only the mirror of herself: what such behavior, if *she* were doing it, would certainly mean. We live in an age and time, besides, where it is virtually impossible to admit without shame that one might prefer the derring-do of Burt Lancaster to the white thighs and ruby lips of a wife. As I prepared Cecilia for bed, I began to dread the scene that awaited me. The snow of the night before—that subtle indicator of change endured—now seemed not so benevolent to me, and the lifting of my penis—an act I had regarded as a mutual recognition and appreciation of irony—struck me as something quite different.

She was sitting at the kitchen counter when I came downstairs, and the dishes, my one remaining distraction, had all been stacked in the dishwasher. The only thing left for me was to add the lemon-scented powder and turn the thing on. Before her was a glass of red wine—a Spanish vintage, highly recommended by our local wine merchant—and the image of her right away struck me as a pose of mourning. It was then that it occurred to me she had come home not to save her marriage but to end it.

I have no idea what my body was doing as it took in this possibility, but I do know that my mind began conducting one of those enormous image-rushes that have always signified to me the onset of panic. Suddenly, a flood of images shot upward, most of them having to do with my old friends, abandonment, and betrayal, until one attained dominance: a vision of the economist Friedman, not as I had most recently imagined him, a pale diminished creature under a hot punishing shower, but hale, hearty, and well-fed at his own dinner table, enjoying a final meal with his wife and two sons, harboring his secret and thinking, as he sopped up the last of the chicken in his wife's good garlic sauce, of the suitcase he would soon pack, and the parking lot of the strip shopping center where he and my wife had no doubt planned, after the twin leave-takings, to meet. Off they would ride into the April evening, most likely to an off-campus motel notorious for its between-classes assignations, to spend a mildly sobering but nonetheless fulfilling evening of committed sex before rising to teach their morning classes.

My great desire at this point was to get out of the room. It was not so much the facts I was resistant to as the melodrama that seemed about to unfold. The garish and eye-popping mode of contemporary domestic warfare has never suited me. It seemed to me altogether better that I should pop into the next room while she composed a note out-

lining her intentions and estimated day and time of depar-
ture. I prefer the thing *written*, that's all, and ambiguity
thereby skirted. If my wife, for instance, is about to say the
words "I'm leaving," what will she *really* be saying? "Fight
for me"? "Don't let me go"? There's no true way of knowing, you see, and in order to find out, I'd have to humiliate
myself in one of those endless groveling scenes I detest.
Whereas if the thing were written down, *typed* even, I'd
have no choice but to accept it.

It would have been a mistake, though, to try to avoid the
scene by preempting her and saying the words myself. I
might have been wrong in my guess, though I didn't think I
was, and any mention of the issue at all would have necessi-
tated our Getting into Things. Leave it covered until you
are forced to uncover it, I say. Meanwhile, as I indulged in
all these speculations, my wife had done nothing but take a
single, maddeningly slow sip of wine. Before the glass had
been replaced in front of her, I announced that I had left
some of Cecilia's toys in the side yard, and used that as an
excuse to get outside.

Ours is a small yard, with just enough room for a few
garden beds and a set of lawn chairs. On summer nights it is
pleasant to sit outside and listen to the crickets, looking up
at the large house with that peculiar sense of pride new
homeowners enjoy. The house is our solidity, the house
and Cecilia asleep within it; all else is a transience too
horrendous to contemplate. In habits such as this, I suppose
I resemble my contemporaries: having lost everything in
the way of surety, we cling to houses and gardens with the
sort of obsessiveness Deborah Kerr once captured so bril-
liantly, when she used to play those fussy and straitlaced
matrons who frittered about in gardens saying things like

"Oh dear! Oh dear! The forsythias are running amuck!" until someone like Burt Lancaster came along to lay her and push her life into a more robust phase. I often think that what we've become is a nation of Deborahs fussing in the garden, waiting for Burt. Who knows what form Burt will take when he comes? Global cataclysm? Religious redemption? It's none of my business, really; I'll either be very old or gone, and it's Cecilia who'll live to find out. I only mention this because it seems to me a comfort to find oneself pitched onto history's plateau, to be alive during one of those insignificant half centuries skipped over in history courses. It was a particular comfort to consider this on an evening when one's wife waited inside the house to end one's marriage. I looked up at the sky, at the clouds covering the moon, and remembered reading once how the astronomer Johannes Kepler thought he heard the lyrics to the music of the spheres, the grinding of the planets forcing out the words "Miseria. Famine. Miseria." But tonight the music of the spheres sounded different to me. What I heard was "Oh dear! Oh dear!" These will be known someday as the Years Before Burt, I thought, and watched as the pale face of the moon slipped out from behind the cover of clouds. How cold it looked. How sad to think of a man standing up on the moon, standing in the middle of a life like mine, staring across the vastness of space at another planet, one assumed empty. Then the image crumbled as I recalled that we had been there, we had confirmed the emptiness. We are now quite certain that no one lives on the moon.

There was a sound from within the house. I turned to see my wife, through the window, washing her wineglass in the sink. Evidently, she'd given up waiting for me. This was not to say that I was off the hook. The monster had submerged, that was all. Meanwhile, my mind, obeying some perverse will of its own, had fallen into a kind of reverie, super-imposing the image of Mrs. Leaver on the woman at the sink. Immediately, I saw it was no good. I am not fool enough to believe that you can put one thing where another belongs and escape that way. My wife was drying her hands. She put her rings—removed for the dish washing—back on, looked out the window once—I knew she wouldn't see me in the darkness—and headed upstairs.

I went and sat on one of the lawn chairs. They are sturdy chairs, a craftsman's chairs, though we bought them cheaply enough, sanded and painted them ourselves. This, again, in the days before Cecilia. We were quite the couple then, quite the doers-of-things-together, and, gathering this information, you will no doubt mark the birth of our child as the end of our romance. That would be the conventional view; it is, I am sure, my wife's view. But as I sat there in the cold chair pondering the end of things, it was not the death of romance that was on my mind; rather, it was the curious happiness I had achieved with Cecilia, a happiness I now saw threatened. As I looked back on the man who had bought and sanded and painted these chairs, I detected a kind of nervousness, an edge, an unfinished quality to him as well. Though he made love to his wife and devoured her meals and lived generally the life of his time, he was, in cer-tain ways, like the man I had imagined before on the moon, encased in an enormous solitude. For some of us, the pres-ence of a woman is not enough to convince us we're not alone. Only a child can do that. And once it happens, all other relations change. There is nothing cruel or deliberate about this; it is simply what happens, simply what is.

I looked at the house then and knew what it was I had to do. It is at such moments that I always wish I smoked cigars, even cigarettes, or drank strong whiskey. There is something pleasing, manly even, in reaching a decision but retaining the presence of mind to finish the smoke or drink in your hand before feeling compelled to act. It attests to the balance of things. But I have none of these vices; there was nothing for me to do, really, but to get up from the chair. Our bedroom window faces the back of the house. From where I was sitting in the side yard, all I could see was the blank wall housing our bedroom, the sloping roof and the eaves. It was up to me to imagine the scene within, without even the helpful scrim of a lit curtain. My wife, who ten minutes ago had left the kitchen, must by then have removed her dress and slipped into a nightgown. There was the ritual of the face cleaning, then the teeth. But I needed only get up. I needed only enter the house. It didn't matter where I found her, really. It would all be the same.

There were first, though, the things a careful husband does before turning in: checking the burners on the gas stove, and the pilot lights; unplugging the coffeemaker; turning down the heat and making sure the lights are out. Then upstairs, quiet against the carpet. My wife was already in bed, asleep, a surprise.

In the bathroom, I undressed. I am either vain or only normally vain, depending on your view of such matters; I give vanity no thought at all, but I do usually take a look at myself naked before turning in. Just as the pilot lights are checked to make sure they're still burning, so the tummy bulge is monitored, and the puffiness around the shoulders and breasts that may be the seat of highest vulnerability in the male. As much as some of us may act or seem to want to act like women, we fear turning into them. We do not want breasts; at least, *I* do not. I don't generally pay too much attention to my genitals, but tonight I studied them, gazed at them like a pile of old schoolbooks I'd just come upon and knew a desire to flip through. They had done their part, like the schoolbooks. One held on to them for nostalgic purposes, and it occurred to me as I regarded them how deeply nostalgia rules our lives after a point, nearly every act a beckoning after an earlier, somehow purer act. What I was about to do was merely a recognition of this truth, an alliance with the world that holds it dear without having any notion of its being a determinant. Nature sees fit to leave us with our genitals even after they have served their function, so we are more or less compelled, for good or ill, to arrange life around their use. This is as far as we have come. Perhaps, I thought as I caught the last ghostly image of myself in the fading of the switched-off light, it is as far as we are capable of going. At least, until Burt comes. Whatever Burt turns out to be.

In bed, I immediately lowered myself to my wife's center. Another nostalgic act, and one I harbored little doubt about. Sex is not difficult even in the worst of times. Certain scents carry on them the film of one's life. In the days when I engaged in this sort of thing regularly, it always seemed to me that, in entering my wife, what I was in fact doing was entering a darkened movie theater and letting the images roll past me, as if it is in sex, not death, that all the important events flash before one's eyes. I don't know if my wife was surprised enough to object when I began to penetrate her; her hands grasped my shoulders, in shock or pleasure I'll never know. The lights were out. She quickly achieved the high moaning that, for me, contained her former presence as acutely as the handwriting of her earliest letters. The difficulty, if there was one, is that studying your wife's early jottings, or her picture in the high school year-book, pleasant as these things might be, is not the same thing as appreciating her presence *now*. So lovemaking had this air for me of a secondary activity, a scratching after the past, a forcible dreaming where real-life, present-tense activity offered too painful an alternative. Yet in this way, and only in this way, I knew I would win her back; the false activity was for her, as for most others, the real. No one is really interested in evolution, or not many. Already, I could feel the onset of the great thwacking orgasm I could always summon from her, loud and deep, a thrumming bass note. And then, always, predictably, her hands would cradle my buttocks, so as to hurry me on, that I might join her in these depths of pleasure, and as I made the first sounds of my own approaching orgasm, her breath became deep and solemn, as if there were something terribly serious about a man let-ting loose a jet of sperm. All of this happened as it had hap-pened in the months and years before, as if we were a pair of old troupers fallen on hard times who had agreed to repeat one of their past successes. Perhaps we would have appeared to any spectator like a pair of ghostly figures on the bed. Or perhaps anyone watching would have thought the scene only just and right: two fine bodies at work, in tune with one another. It was perfect sex, really, the kind we all aspire to. And I am just smart enough to admit that about all the important matters I may be dead wrong. Per-haps this was precisely what we ought to have been doing, and no more.

Afterward, my wife cradled close to me, affectionately. I

trust there is not an excess of vanity in the fact that, for me, at that moment, there was no question as to the defeat of the economist Friedman. I was aware of him fading, of the light closing around us and on this image of domestic restoration. Not for nothing do we respond as we do to the fifth acts of Shakespeare's romances. No one, even in this unlikely age, is fond of divorce. The notion persists that certain people belong together, and I am content to believe this is so for us. I waited until she was asleep and then went into Cecilia's room.

There is not a lot there. We are neither of us much for the sorts of painted-ceilinged wonderlands you see in the movies when the filmmakers want very badly to let you know how devoted the young parents are. Most babies live in rooms like prisons, and gaze out at the world through the bars of a crib. None of this is accidental. Life, in fact, is extraordinarily blank: rooms have walls and floors, that's all, Cecilia, and this is where we live, here, between these walls and floors, in these rooms, and with luck we can keep them blank, keep away the terrible scenes and fights that require us, in reaction, to pin up pleasant scenes and vistas that are all of a piece with falseness. None of this, of course, will I ever tell her. Instead, I will pat her small tender head and invent stories and tales like any other father. Only in silence will I offer the enormous thanks that is due her. This little room is my chalice, my cathedral, of course; I'm not telling you anything new in admitting to this. I will do what I can to preserve it. I will do what I must to retain my happiness.

THE LAKE

My name is Danny Sienkewicz. I am a firefighter in Denniston, Massachusetts, a town with just over 15,000 inhabitants and little to speak of in the way of a commercial district. Needless to say, we don't fight a lot of fires here. Since no major highway runs through our town, neither will you find us called more than four or five times a week to assist at an emergency.

Recently, however, we had a tragedy at the station. The wife of one of the firefighters died. He killed her, accidentally. Timmy McCandles. But right away, having said that—having used the word *tragedy*—I want to back off from it. When I hear that word spoken, I can't help it, my mind goes directly back to the image of Mrs. Carney, my teacher in junior-year English at Denniston High. Mrs. Carney said death didn't count as tragedy unless the person who died might have achieved greatness. And this sunk in for me, I remembered. So let me say instead, we had a sadness not long ago at the station. The men, though, all insist on referring to it as a tragedy, and I never contradict them. Though I know more than any of them what actually happened, I maintain my silence, and allow them to use whatever words they want.

I am a married man. I did not go to college. My father was not a firefighter. Instead, he was one of those men who fought in Korea and came home and begot children and drank too much and ended up in the Old Soldiers' Home, dying of a rotting liver and wasted lungs, both at the same time; the race was to see which would get him first. I think it was the lungs, but then, I stopped paying attention at a certain point. I have this image of myself in high school, around the time of my father's death. I am sitting in a classroom full of thugs, and girls ready at a second's notice to get pregnant by them, and then those few who are taking notes and preparing for college. I am not going crazy with hormones or thinking about sleeping with these girls or about going to college, either, though I suppose I could have, I was told I had the aptitude. I am, instead, fixed on a point outside the room. The life I am going to live has become clear to me; I have fashioned it, though I am only seventeen at the time. I will have a wife and children, three or four of them; I will have a certain house, with trimmed hedges, and on Saturdays you will see me out there, like all the other men, in a tee shirt and scuffed, faintly dirty khakis, trimming and pruning. I envisioned things with an orderliness I imagined my father could never so much as approximate from his chair at the Old Soldiers' Home. I saw myself all grown up, packing the children in the car and going on picnics. And I knew, even then, how I would look in that car, my eyes staring straight ahead at all times, never quite fixing on what's on either side of me.

You have to admire me for this, I achieved my goal. When I was done with Cadet School, I began looking at girls, and not until then, at least not with any seriousness. I went on living with my mother after Cadet School; my two older sisters were married, the opportunities were not great. I loved my life in those days, my rituals, swimming at the Y every night, but it was hard to meet girls. So here is an embarrassment: Sharon, my wife, lived two doors down the street; I'd known her since childhood. What I knew about her at that time was that she'd become a nurse and gotten engaged, but something had gone wrong, the galoot she was going to marry got in a motorcycle accident, lost some vital function. Sharon held on for a while, but it was no good. In the neighborhood, we knew such stories of loyalty and hard luck. Watching Sharon go in and out of the house in her white sneakers and hose I felt a pity in my heart, and in my imagination began to place her inside the picture I'd formed in high school: the trimmed shrubs, the packed car. I started going over to her house, I found excuses. I don't remember love, but that did not seem important then. When we first slept together, I thought this woman exuded milk, it was like being an infant again, and the sensation I had was of dipping myself in an enormous, brimming bowl. She was, at the beginning, one who was prone to cry after lovemaking, and I did not ask, but assumed this was grief over the lost motorcyclist. I felt, holding this crying woman in my arms in the backseat of my car, that something quite natural was going on, a transference: if I held her and said nothing for a long enough time, she would stop loving him and start loving me—or she would, at the very least, and good enough, *accept* me—and that is what I believed, for a long time, happened.

Our girls are three and four. We've rested now, but next year we'll have a boy. I know this as certainly as I once knew I would reach this life of mine. We have boys' names picked out. Duncan or Griffin or maybe just Joe. I joke with Sharon about this, how the classrooms in four or five years aren't going to have any normal names left. "Let's do our part," I joke to Sharon. "Let's people the world with Joes." She laughs and goes along with me, but then she gets that look that tells me she'd be fine stopping here, with just the girls. It's a snag we've hit, Sharon and I, and though I don't believe this is an obstruction that will last forever, I would be a fool not to admit that Lisa's death put it there.

Timmy, Lisa's husband, has been my best friend since high school, when he shone at baseball and I failed to distinguish myself in the hundred-yard dash. I knew Timmy's flaws early, though I forgave him them. Or maybe it's truer to say I never considered them as being separate from him. He was always more handsome than me and less capable of sustained effort, more prone to sullenness and moods, which around here, given his Irishness, always meant that he would drink hard. Lisa chose him when he was at his peak, when he still had his fastball, his redheaded good looks, and a breezy, young man's confidence that could knock you over. It soon became their joke, at the high school cafeteria table, to confide in the rest of us just enough of the details of their passion to drive us all crazy. "Was it cookies or cake this weekend?" someone would ask them at Monday lunch, "cookies" and "cake" being, of course, code words for the two basic things teenagers knew to do then. Lisa wore a flushed look in those days, her maturity starting up in her, and she had a way of looking across the table at Timmy, as if knowing even then that he was going to fuck up, going to be her burden in the years to come, but this had been her training: to find some flawed man and carry him.

As for me, I sat and studied them, as if they were light-years away from me, as if what they had together was only possible for certain rare species, and even for them would always be touch-and-go. The bulk of my affection—certainly my attention—at that time was reserved for Timmy's father. He was the fire chief. He knew how to drink in moderation and had a passion for watering his lawn. I stood and watched him, every chance I got, because in the look of his resting old man's face as he moved about his yard in the summer dusk, in his careful and methodical manner with the hose, I felt as close to a form of teaching as I have ever received from any man. I think he was aware of this, too, and allowed me to see, those nights, the core belief that kept him steady in his days: the purest part of life, its aching, gorgeous center, was a thing deeply mired in the past. It was useless to try to seize that sweetness, because it was already, at the moment he and I were born, played out. But distillations of it, of the life some lucky bastard had once gotten to live, came down from the air sometimes, onto lawns, into backyards, in certain kinds of light, and your goal as a man must be to position yourself so that these landed on you.

The decision to become a firefighter occurred on one of those nights when I sat alone in a lawn chair in the McCandleses' backyard. Timmy had stepped inside to get us each a soft drink, and his father had gone deep into his yard. The Chief was standing under an apple tree, looking up into it. He was muttering something at the time, and it had a sullen and half-angry tone to it. The yard was narrow but long. The Chief seemed to have planted everything there: apple and peach trees, a grape arbor. It was May and the air was that thick. Chief McCandles looked in my direction and I'm sure did not see me. The sound of his muttering might have reached someone else in a different way, might have sounded like an unhappiness any boy would want to run from. His life, I knew, was imperfect. Still, it seemed to me then as desirable as anything a human being should aspire to. I would go one step further and say that what I understood, at that moment, was that human beings shouldn't desire perfection, but only to take their necessary woes into arbors, into sweet-smelling manmade enclosures. So there it was: Timmy came out with the drinks, and I had made what was to be the major decision of my life.

It took me four years, though, to save up for what Timmy got on graduation: the six months' freedom to go off and study hose hydraulics and qualify for an EMT. In those four years, I stood as Timmy's best man, I held his baby daughter, Erin, at the font while the priest poured holy water on her head. I even became Erin's baby-sitter in a pinch, and learned how to change a diaper and hold an infant high on your shoulder so her stomach settles. Often, on those nights when I was usually so tired I fell asleep before they came home, I would be awakened by Lisa's hand on my shoulder, where there might be a spit-up stain left by Erin, and I can still recall that first bleary vision of Lisa above me as I came into wakefulness, a woman who had recently grown tired, saying, "Wake up, Danny," very gently, while behind her, Timmy stood, having drunk a little too much on their date and ready now to give me the boot so that he could get Lisa into the bedroom. Lisa's hand, meanwhile, rested on my wet shoulder a little longer than it strictly needed to, and I believe a sympathy started up between us then.

I suppose I became less available to them as time went on. I finally saved up enough so that my mother would be all right while I went off to Cadet School, then found myself inserted, by stealth, by the complex network of allegiances that extend over two counties here, in a neighboring city's ladder company. "We'll wait for something to turn up in Denniston." Chief McCandles winked. I could wait. Most nights found me waist-deep in the YMCA pool, surveying the room for the girl I would marry. There were nights when Timmy insisted on accompanying me, just to get out of the house, I think. He would stand beside me in the water, giving off signs of envy at my bachelor state, assuming, when I looked at women, he knew what was on my mind. But Timmy, by then, no longer received my intimacies—we'd grown past all that—so he couldn't know how, when women walked through the door of the Y, tucking their hair into caps, wet from their pre-swim showers, it wasn't sexual availability I sought, but something more specific, a quality I was later to find in Sharon, my wife. There was a certain walk, a manner of tucking the hair, a composure and a sense of banked hopes that were for me, in those days, the very composition of desire. After our swims and showers, when we sat together in the bar, I didn't mention any of this to Timmy. Instead, I listened. It was no different from what I'd always done, allowed Timmy's life to be the important one. By then a string of complaints had started to flow from him, all that Lisa wasn't. I sat and waited for the moment when he would tell me he didn't love her anymore, at which point I would rise and, in my mind's eye anyway, punch him in the face.

I drove him home those nights, and I always waited at the foot of their driveway until he made it to the door. More often than not, Lisa would come outside before he got there, like she'd been looking out for him. There was physical contact between them, though of an uninterpretable sort: Timmy, who had so recently complained of her coldness, always reached out for her with a kind of loping, heartsick movement; she reached back, and the words he had spoken to me in the bar had this immediate tendency to fade. Somebody tells you their story, that's not their story, I always thought, watching them. Hers was a vaguer touch than his, certainly, but they were always together when I drove off, together in a way that seemed theirs alone, keeping the same sort of secret they'd kept at the cafeteria table. Was it going to be cookies tonight, or cake? Driving away from them, I found myself doing something I very rarely did—that is, looking at both sides of the road, into the thick woods surrounding their house, as if something lay in waiting there for me to discover, something I both wished for and feared.

Such feelings, however, had usually dissipated by morning. They did not, in any case, cause me to relax my vigilance. I found and married Sharon, and nine months and four days later we had the first of our baby girls. After the first was born, we waited three months and conceived the second, all according to a plan that existed in my head and that Sharon, in her pliant and docile manner, never once raised her voice against.

⊠

Just a few months after Sharon got pregnant for the second time, Lisa found herself pregnant, too. It was too much of a coincidence for me to believe Timmy wasn't being competitive. What was Lisa to him in those days? They'd gotten to acting surly in each other's company. Lisa had finally finished up her degree in physical therapy and had gone back to work. She wanted to wait a couple more years before having a kid, or maybe—who knows?—stop at Erin, and Timmy wasn't fond of that idea at all. So within three months of each other, Sharon gave birth to our second daughter, Erica, and Lisa had Pete.

When Erica was a year old, I began putting up a swing set in the yard. Here, we work three days on, three days off, so there were a lot of days when I was home, hot afternoons spent putting in the concrete footings, and being home that much, I began to notice the baby was crying a lot. Annoyed, I'd go inside the house to check on things and find Sharon in bed, while Maryann, our elder daughter, sat in front of the TV and the baby stood screaming in her crib. "What is it?" I'd ask Sharon, and she'd just look at me from the bed, drawn and pale, and like she wished I knew enough not to have to ask such a question. I'd go and get the baby and try to soothe her, then bring her to Sharon. Sharon would take her from me, all right, but a part of her just wasn't there.

It was Lisa who had to tell me, finally. "She's depressed, Danny." I hated that word. It was a word I wanted to dance away from. Lisa sat there, patient, waiting for me to come back. She told me later my head did a thing, the sort of motion a dog makes, somber and terribly still, when he knows he's about to be punished. "It happens," she said, with some gentleness I was grateful for.

It certainly hadn't happened to Lisa. She'd joined a gym

after Pete was born, and taken off all the creamy, pleasing weight her body had taken on during two pregnancies. I guess it wasn't pleasing to her. She talked a lot about going back to work as soon as Pete was old enough, and she was filled with a crazy kind of energy that, beside my insomnia-bred state, sometimes felt vaguely annoying.

I couldn't sleep beside Sharon anymore: the fact of her going away distressed me too deeply. But I hadn't the beginning of an idea what to do about it. I'd thought making love a lot would be a way of rousing Sharon, bringing her back from the dead, but it only succeeded in making her go further away. She'd stopped responding to me, or else she'd respond too late, in a way that let me know she was pretending. Then she'd fall asleep right afterward, like the fakeness of it didn't bother her one bit.

For a while, Sharon's mother helped out with child care, but she did it grumpily. So it was a problem. And then one day Lisa said, "Let me take the baby. I'm home anyway, with Pete. It's no problem. Let's let Sharon get some rest."

Sharon never objected to this. She may have only pulled the covers closer to her chin when I proposed it, and retreated into those dreams of hers. I agreed, because I didn't know what else to do. I put Maryann in day care and drove Erica to Lisa's every day I didn't have to go on shift. And on the days when I did, Lisa came and picked up Erica herself.

The way things worked out, it never seemed too much of an intrusion on Lisa's time. She was always full of that manic energy on those days when I came to drop Erica off. It was like she was fueled by a force toward something, though what that could be, in the house, in the baby-smelling rooms, in our little town, was out of my power to guess. She was frequently on the phone, and motioned that

I should put Erica down and just go, she could handle things. But I didn't feel right about that. Sometimes I brought Erica into the living room, where Pete was on the floor, messing with his teething rings or trying to grab their scruffy cat, and the two of them would play so well together I'd lie down on the couch and catch up on my sleep right there.

Often, I'd wake up an hour later and find Lisa and the babies sitting at the dining room table, having a snack and laughing at me. "You snore something awful, Danny," Lisa would say. I wasn't embarrassed, she'd caught me sleeping too many times in my life. She was like my sister, and though we'd had a careful physical relationship since high school, I retained, looking at her, some old sense of having taken baths together as children, a shared innocence that could not be broached. I was not quite a man in Lisa's presence, but someone on his way to becoming one. If it was early enough when I woke and we neither of us had to race to pick up our older kids, mine from day care and hers from kindergarten, I'd offer to watch the babies and let her get in an extra hour at the gym. She always took me up on it, too, and sometimes, when things were going especially well in this new arrangement of ours, I became ambitious, and told Lisa she could get out more if she wanted. I even told her if she needed to go back to work a couple of times a week, I thought I could handle it. I could watch the babies on the days I wasn't working.

"You want to be my husband, Danny?" she said when I offered all this to her, and it had a light, ridiculous sound to it that was actually a relief to me. I was aware I might be trying to step into Timmy's shoes—not as lover, never that—but as he should have worn them, taking responsibility for what she might need. And I was careful about it, too. I only stayed with Lisa on the days when he was on shift. If he happened to be home, I never intruded, just dropped Erica off and skedaddled, let them have whatever they still had together.

One afternoon, Lisa and I were standing in the kitchen. Pete had just thrown up all over himself and she was worried he was sick. She had big, overblown worries about Pete, always. She'd taken off his clothes and begun to soak them in the sink. There were already dirty dishes there. I was holding Pete and she was trying to soak his clothes without moving the dishes and her movements seemed to me not properly thought out, even stupid. I handed her Pete and I got out a basin and filled it and soaked the clothes and then, very proud of myself, said, "There," and looked up at her. I caught something then, though I didn't at first want to; my reaction was to look back at the soaking clothes and maybe rearrange them. When I turned back to her, it was still there, though now covered some, it would have to be, because such intensity can't just hang out there, it would scorch, or get scorched. But it made things uncomfortable for about ten minutes. Really, we'd just made love. It doesn't always happen in beds, or in cars, the way people think it does, with clothes off, with organs and hands. It happens sometimes in rooms, while the man has his hand in a tub of sopping baby clothes and the woman is holding a naked infant. A thing passes, very strong, the very thing that *gets* you into bed, and the other catches it, registers, and things between two people are forever changed.

There was no chance, though, that Lisa and I were going to stay away from one another after that. Maybe we didn't know enough to be scared. Instead, I took Pete and she washed her hands and went and did something else, not even in another room, right there in the kitchen; maybe wet a washcloth to cool down Pete's body. I had him in my arms and I could feel how hot he was, how hot and unhappy. We went ahead and did our chores, just like it was any day.

And it *was* any day, or could have been, when it finally happened, a day when both Erica and Pete took their naps at the same time, and without either of us saying anything about it, we went into the bedroom and fucked. I say "fucked" because I don't know any other word for it, because I closed off my mind, drew a curtain over it, from the moment I took her hand and led her in. Otherwise, I don't know how I could have done it, let go of caution that way.

I don't have any memories of those times, at least not of the first six months. I couldn't describe them to you now. Maybe that's true of all sex that matters: you try to dive back to the thing, the touch or the lick, that incited feeling in you, and you realize it came from somewhere else. I was aware, from the start, of two things: of everything about it being wrong, and everything about it mattering, in a way I had not known such things could matter before. I didn't like this, but I followed it. I split my life in two. In the station, I made my little jokes, and laughed at the jokes of others. I did the shopping and tended to the house and went on making love to Sharon in a dim, hopeful way, and in all of these acts was a certain kind of conviction as well. I think during this time my hopes for Sharon's return went unabated, as though that would fix things somehow. Sometimes, only sometimes, picking up a can off a supermarket shelf, I might feel my knees go weak under me for a second, and my hands grip the handles of the shopping cart until they were white, and I'd think, at these moments, that a price was about to be exacted. I'd almost welcome this, but it would pass. I'd put the can in the cart, I'd touch my daughter's hair if one of them happened to be seated in the cart, and we'd push on to the next aisle. It would be a day.

The story I told myself, for six months, about our fucking, was that Lisa was an unhappy woman and that I might have been anyone. Not anyone. But I might have been any number of men who sat and listened, who seemed gentle, who weren't Timmy.

What assisted this was that we didn't talk much, really, for six months. She'd scratch my chest afterward, a long, subtle gesture. At the end, it was not so subtle, it began to hurt, like she'd been digging into me. I thought to myself at such moments: if Timmy'd just let her work, this wouldn't be happening. Behind the house, their yard went on and on. Timmy had bought big, his father had helped him. They were half a mile from their nearest neighbor and Timmy envisioned stables. But he never put in a fence. I'd get up from the bed, I'd put on my shorts—because to stand naked in front of her was still too embarrassing—and I'd look out into that yard, imagining what I'd have put there, thinking: if Timmy just cared about his yard a little more . . . Even when Lisa told me once how she'd started loving me when she'd seen me so gentle with baby Erin, I didn't hear that, or chose not to hear it. The word *love* stood out too much; it sounded wrong, it was something we never talked about, and so I buried it.

But then one day I was getting up from the bed and she pulled me back down. I thought I was going to hit her, I was in that moment so angry; I could sense some new, complicated demand on its way to being made, and I was on guard for it. She pulled me down and I thought what I was being asked to do was make love to her again, which I was ready to do, though angrily. That wasn't what she wanted. She wanted me to look at her. And when I did, she burst into tears. Her face looked all bunched up and ugly, and it held a message in it, unmistakable.

Because I didn't want to hear or see Lisa's message, I made love to her again, in my habitual way, only she made none of the little sounds that told me: now this, and then this. She was crying, whimpering really, and it took me back to Sharon, those early nights in the car when she, too, would cry, and I'd say to myself: hold on and your life is made. But here, Lisa's crying had an opposite effect on me. At a certain point, I stopped, I looked at her, I felt the way she was holding me. I heard some voice from far off telling me where I was. It was no surprise. I will not put a name on this moment, or on the knowledge I attained then, except to say that after that afternoon, the change I had dreaded at last came about. That is, the conviction with which I had attended to chores, attended to my wife, had left me, and these gestures became empty ones.

It was a blessing during this time that Sharon had ceased to need me. But nobody stays lucky forever. One night we were in the house and I was frolicking some with the kids, getting them ready for bed. Sharon, as always, was lying down, and I dipped into the bedroom and made a joke, my good mood spilling over to her, and watched her smile. In some remote, unaffected corner, I wished her well; wished even, out of long habit, for her recovery. Then I went back to the girls. Erica was easy enough to get to sleep, but Maryann required a long story. I sat in the rocking chair and rocked and read her something—"Rikki-Tikki-Tavi," I think—and practically fell asleep myself. Then I tucked her in and went into the bedroom and lay beside Sharon.

The lights were on downstairs but I was too tired to go down there and shut them off. I thought I'd just go to sleep and leave them blazing. I had only my gym shorts on, as I recall. Suddenly I felt her hand on my chest, a thing I hadn't felt there in a long time. She stroked and stroked and I tried to read her gesture, tried to see it as a thing in time and space requiring a thoughtful response. She kept doing it so long I almost fell asleep under it, but then she was stroking my belly and finally her hand went under my shorts. I woke up then. The next thing was Sharon was climbing on top of me, doubly surprising because that had never been her preferred position. I hoped she had the diaphragm in, because I found in that instant that I no longer wanted Joe. I shut my eyes and listened to her take her pleasure from out of some closed, protected place inside of which I'd locked myself.

After that, whenever I made love to Lisa, certain feelings I'd had inside her body, real but until then somehow ignorable, grew large, as though they wanted very much for me to see them; as though, too, they knew they were in danger of being lost. There were moments, inside her, when I had the sensation of surfacing on a lake, my skin wet and supple, opening my eyes and surveying a spread of water and a setting of hills I could not recall having actually seen in my life. Maybe I was there in childhood and was only now recalling it, but I didn't think so. In fact, I seemed to know, in some bottled-up part of my brain, just what was happening to me, and what the lake was.

Almost as soon as Sharon recovered, another thing happened. Timmy and I were sitting in the station one day. I'd been moved to Denniston just a few months before, so we shared a shift now and then, not often. I was studying for my promotion exam in *Kirk's Fire Investigation*, had the book open to a certain page, and Timmy came over and ran his finger down the page, made a long smudgy crease in the middle of it. He was standing behind me, rubbing up close against my back, so close I felt this impulse to shove him away, and while I was experiencing this feeling and looking at the smudge he'd made, I got it. I got what was happening. It was like he knew, too, because he moved away, he began talking to somebody else. I watched him, saw the slant of Timmy's body against the light coming in through the firehouse window, and I became afraid. If Timmy could do that simple thing to me, it seemed there was nothing he couldn't do. I was afraid if we had to go to a fire he'd find a way of killing me there. I went back to the book, I tried to study the page, but it was no good. The whole story was in front of me now, the way what Lisa and I were doing was wrong, the way my surfacing on the hidden lake was one side of a movie set, on the other side of which Timmy expected to find somebody who was never going to meet him there. I looked at Timmy and tried to love him the way I once had, and though this was difficult, it awakened something in me that I think was glad to be awakened.

Lisa and I had to begin talking then. We had to begin *discussing*. I insisted on it. We talked first about Pete, and she told me something she'd never said before: how Pete had been born out of a wrong guess, that she'd stopped loving Timmy by the time Pete was conceived and so had never learned to love Pete properly. She was afraid he'd die because of it, she'd seen that sign on his fore-head all his little life. We stopped talking then, for a while, it was too sad, too dark. I think we embarrassed ourselves with it. But soon we had to start in again, this time about Timmy knowing, and what that meant, and each time we had that conversation I'd get out of bed and stalk the room, and always when I did that I'd put something on, but she'd stay in bed, naked and not ashamed to be. That was Lisa: she wasn't afraid to see things just as they were, but me, I always wanted to make them into other, safer things.

Finally, what happened was, one afternoon, just over four months ago, I told Lisa I wouldn't be coming anymore. She bit her lip and said, "I know," but at the same time did not believe me. So I kept coming for another week. I had lost conviction, though, and I pushed away the image of the lake and kept my eyes open and saw instead the sheets, curtains, the way her face was aging and how hard it would be to love a woman for just this, when the facts were age and death. When I thought this, the lower half of my heart felt sub-merged in something acidic. I had the vague sense of going against nature and that this was possible, a choice. "Of course, we couldn't," she said once, and I was glad to hear it, to hear her thinking that way, too; it made me believe the old world, the world of the cafeteria table, could be restored.

What I did in the end was just stop coming. Sharon was well enough now, and no longer needed the help, so there was no longer the problem of Erica, who had anyway stopped taking naps. I went ahead and sewed up my life. I thought about conceiving Joe, the process of which had begun in a haphazard fashion. At the station, I even announced it once, at lunch, said we might be trying again and we wanted a boy, and Zgrodnik, a twenty-year veteran, said, with his mouth full of egg, "It's who wants it most." I raised my eyebrows. "What determines the sex. If the man wants it more, it's always a girl."

One night I happened to be home watching television with Sharon when the phone rang. It was raining hard, and what I hoped was that I wasn't being called in to work because someone had gotten sick and the crew was short. It was Lisa. She was crying, or in a state like that. Maybe not crying. She was alone. Timmy was working. She said she needed to see me.

I heard that and I listened to the rain on the roof and wondered, in my detached way, how long the roof was going to last and when we were going to have to go in for the expense of repairing it. I have this way of thinking double, when there's something I don't really want to hear, and I put it to use. In the other room, I heard the TV, the comedy, the laugh track, and waited for Sharon to say, "Who is it?" and then, when she didn't, thought of her sitting there, absorbed in some little comedy full of people in bright clothes and plastic hair, while here was Lisa, desperate on the other end of the line, and all I could think was how Sharon's world was preferable—watching TV, staying in our lives, these things were better. Lisa needed to see that, the whole pitch of our lives just needed to be adjusted, that was all, like turning a knob and bringing things into a clearer, better focus.

"Park away from the house," Lisa said. "Please, Danny. On the road.

"Away from the house," she repeated, and I thought that was strange.

"Why?"

"I think Timmy's got somebody watching. Just turn off your lights and I'll be looking for you."

That sounded calculated, and when I put it alongside the hysteria I almost didn't go. What could happen, after all? Sobs, tears, and maybe a blow job. It had descended to that, that's how cold I felt. I didn't want to see Lisa anymore. But I went. I believe my excuse to Sharon was that a couple of air packs had been misplaced down at the station and I couldn't direct the men to them on the phone. Something that lame.

When I reached the house, I parked a long way down the road. Maybe she wouldn't find me and I would have my excuse. "I was there, and you didn't find me." I could see through the woods the lights in their house. They were the only lights around. I was sitting in a parked car in the dark, listening to the rain, and wondering if my car would get stuck because theirs was an unpaved road, muddy and deserted. And I have to say this, too, because it was a part of the night: I'd begun to feel safe again. I'd begun to feel that things were going to be all right, restored. Lisa was going to be hysterical for a while, and then she was going to be Lisa again. I remember thinking that, and though it was rainy and dark, a kind of warmth started up in me. I sat there and I thought she would probably come, probably find me, we would have some sex but it wouldn't count, we were on the other side of all its weight and importance. I could barely remember the lake. As I thought that, I remember smiling, almost like I was anticipating the sex, and I did this thing, embarrassing to admit, I cupped my balls in my hand and looked down at them, just interested and anticipatory, and at that moment something came into my mind, a little shadow came flying in and perched there, a contradictory shadow that told me the way I was thinking wasn't the way it was. When I looked up, it was like Lisa had risen directly out of this sensation, so that I couldn't force it away but had to stare right into it. If I'd stopped to analyze things, I might have wondered why her face was lit that way, but I didn't ask that, of course. I just saw. And what I saw was Lisa wet and excited, running toward Danny. Toward *Danny*. I had to take that in, maybe for the first time. That I was loved. For a single moment, before I had the chance to stop myself, I was ready to have my life change, and hers too, because of it. I lifted toward that sweet thing there in the car, and felt a dark place in me start to open. And then the whole reason Lisa's face was lit announced itself: it was a car coming.

My first thought was: it would pass, we'd both go back to what it was we'd been ready for in the moment before, the little leap we'd both been preparing to make. This was an intrusion, that was all—blink, and it'd be over. Except the car didn't pass. Instead, it slammed into Lisa—her face knew enough to be frightened for a moment just before— and I saw right away it was Timmy's truck. She had disappeared from my sight, I was looking at the taillights of Timmy's truck and the nozzle of a big gas can leaning over the side. I saw Timmy jump out of the cab and then I heard the amazing sound of Timmy howling.

That sound was like nothing I'd ever heard before, not like the howl you hear when people think they're going to die. More like the sound inside caves, that sound of essential, bedrock loneliness. I didn't stop to think it was strange, the way that howl made everything else take second place. It was like, after hitting her with the truck, the first thing he wanted to offer up—to me, to her—was an intimacy greater than any he'd offered either of us before: this is how much I feel, you bastards. I'm still here, and I feel *this much*.

It's stupid to say it made me forgive him, but the thing it did that I have trouble understanding is the way it stood between me and what he had done. For several seconds, I was outside of any thought of revenge or anger. I was just listening to him.

I did get out of the car finally. I went and watched how he was holding her, and it was like those nights I used to drop him off after drinking. Like it was their lives, after all, and I had no business. I could see that Lisa was dead, but I still shouted did he want me to make the call. He just motioned for me to get the hell away, so there was no arguing with him. He did it over and over again, and I knew there was no place for me there anymore.

So I got back in the car and only on the ride home did I start to think of the realness of it, of Lisa being dead. I felt ashamed of myself when I realized how long it had taken me to think about this. And there was something else, too: while I'd been listening to Timmy howl, there had been another thought, one I could barely admit to. I kept batting it away, but though it had been there only for a second, it had lodged in my memory. I might almost call it gratefulness, for what her death meant, what it meant I didn't have to do.

I wasn't going to tell Sharon when I got home. I couldn't imagine speaking anything of it, or doing anything but lying down and falling into a deep, blank sleep. Sharon was still watching television, though, and I was lucky: only ten minutes after I got home the call came from the station, saying that Timmy McCandles had accidentally run over his wife, in the rain, outside their house.

So we went to a funeral. We left our little girls with Sharon's mother and I put on my one black suit and Sharon a dark blue dress and we sat in the fourth row at St. Ignatius's. There was all the predictable sobbing and a lot of grim men who were firefighters. Friends of Timmy's, friends of the Chief's. In the front row, Erin sat next to her father. Someone had fixed her hair up carefully, in dark barrettes. Timmy had done the following: after I'd driven away that night, he'd taken their second car, the Bronco, and parked it where my car had been. He claimed Lisa had left the car out there and was going to fetch something from it when he'd come upon her, unaware, and slid into her. He was just coming home, that was all. He claimed his whole intention had been to pick up some spices, some hot sauce and Worcestershire; he was due to cook that night, for the men. Somehow the trackings in the mud managed to match up to that story. Or maybe they hadn't looked hard enough. It had been a rainy night, remember, and ours is a county with strong, old allegiances. So it was a tragic accident, you see.

For me, by this time, Timmy's howl had ceased to make the terrible sense it had made that night. By now, I was able to see the calculation in what Timmy had done, though I would never, ever speak of it. I couldn't see what good it would do anymore, and Timmy, since the night of the accident, had aged to the point where he looked as old as his father. So I knew some kind of punishment was going on.

Every once in a while I would think of Lisa as she had

been in life, and how, because of me, she was dead. There was nowhere to go with that thought—it was just a dark place inside me that I knew I would have to learn to live with. I knew, too, though I couldn't guess yet what effect it would take, that Lisa's death would finally put a mark on me as great as the mark it had put on Timmy.

Last night—it's been three months now, it's already summer—I went out to take care of the lilacs. The blooms are gone, and I'm just getting the lime in. It's late for that, but I have to do it, and it'll be in for next year. I have three beautiful lilac bushes in my backyard, a dogwood, a mountain ash. I have the yard I always wanted, the yard I dreamed of when I was a boy, and as I sifted around the roots of the lilac, I had this moment of remembering. It was a June night, I could hear kids somewhere not far off. I was scratching in the earth and I was aware that the clothes I was wearing, the tee shirt and khakis, the pose and the physical attitude, these were nearly exactly what I'd once envisioned for myself in the old, hopeful, planning days, and I thought in that instant that if I could have gone back and been, at the same time, the boy dreaming this life and the man living it, how happy I'd have been.

What I did, though, is I looked up and saw Sharon staring at me from the porch. The porch loses the light early and she was standing in shadow. I caught her face, though. I tried to smile and she didn't smile back. I'd caught Sharon thinking. It's a way she's started to look lately, a pensiveness that's set in in the months since Lisa died. It was automatic that I looked from her face to her belly and wondered if Joe was in there yet. It was very clear at that moment—I'm not sure why—that he wasn't. I went back to her face. We stared across a great space at one another and I wondered what she might be thinking. But it has become Sharon's determination, these last few months, not to let me know. She went deeper into the shadows. I hesitated a moment. I looked around my yard and saw my hand white from the lime, and I thought, very clearly, of the game of my life as being lost. But then I went on, as I do every day, just as if it wasn't.

LOVE, YOUR PARENTS

I am thirty-four years old. Two weeks ago, I came home to live with my parents in the big house they built for themselves on the banks of the Severn River. I brought with me two suitcases of clothes and the '81 Datsun I drive. Everything else, I threw out when I left Belchertown, where I lived once with my wife and son, and then more recently with my girlfriend. There is a joke somewhere in all of this, and any minute now I expect to get it. When I do, I will release one of those tiny hiccuping laughs of mine, short and to the point. My girlfriend used to tell me it scared her to hear me laugh like that, and my wife went further, said I had a sociopath's laugh, that I didn't know how to let go but always kept my eyes open in the midst of laughter, so that no one, not even the jokester in front of me, could get the better of me.

All of which may be true, but it doesn't concern me.

It's wet outside as I sit here, a morning in late May turning hot after last night's rain. Downstairs, my mother will already have breakfast on. She won't keep me company, though, when I'm ready to eat it. It's hard for her to sit in the house with me now, in my come-down-in-the-world state. Pretty soon I'll hear her pull her car out of the garage; then I'll know I've got the house to myself. What I'll do is I'll call my girlfriend—you see I don't waste time: sixteen days home and already I've got one—and arrange when we can meet today, and where. I do let go one of the hiccuping laughs when I think about this. I imagine my girlfriend Cathy describing what we're having as a "whirlwind courtship." What other way is there for her to talk about this guy who comes to her out of the blue and wants to see her every day? I told her I'm a screenwriter here to do research. "A love story set on the Maryland coast," I told her. She's my therapist's secretary, so someday she'll find me out and this will be over. But I imagine I have a while to go; these guys are supposed to keep their patients' secrets, and my hunch is that Dr. Petticord takes this sort of injunction very seriously.

I'm doing the therapy based on Currey's advice. Currey was my supervisor up north. He told me it had been helping him get through the most difficult time of his life, and he believed it might help me too. (Actually, his words were a bit stronger, and included the phrase "to avoid criminal prosecution," which I have to say, in Currey's favor, came out sounding all garbled and insincere.) I arrived here with 800 bucks, and though technically this is supposed to go for child support, my wife will have to fight me to get it. By the time the long arm of the law reaches my outpost on the Severn, I'll have spent most of it; sixty bucks a shot on therapy, gas for the car, insurance, meals with Cathy—these are my expenses. When it's all used up, I'll be in that tight spot where I have to ask my parents for money. But I won't think about that yet.

Though all this money business might sound lousy on balance, in fact I'm hurting no one. My wife comes from money. The demand for child support is her way of getting me to pay for something that doesn't need to be paid for. She wanted a child. But somehow that isn't enough for her. My wife wants me to have wanted one, too, and the fact that I never did is what keeps her fired up. A man who doesn't care about his own kid—or doesn't care in a way she can understand—is not a man she could have married. The converse, I guess, in her view, is that if I pay the support I become caring. Some part of her will settle for that, anyway. But the truth is a shade different. A little hand shot out of her when she started with me, started grabbing things. The wild little grasping hand that rises directly out of hunger. She's ashamed of that now, wants me to tell her, by my actions, that things were different. But that's not my way.

I mentioned my old supervisor Currey a while back, but what I neglected to mention is that, soon before I left, Currey found out that his wife had cancer all over her body. Here was this gorgeous radiant woman who'd come around the Home a few times, and the next thing you know, everybody's whispering how she's dying. You could tell from looking at Currey the day the rumor came out that it was true, too. He's a small, wiry kind of guy whose body has an athletic sort of quickness to it; I had him pegged the first day I saw him, the day I came in for the interview. I

asked who would be interviewing me and they pointed out
Currey, and it was then that I decided what my history
would be. I played two years of pro ball, I wrote on the
application form. The Cincinnati Bengals, I decided for no
good reason. I look like I could have played ball, and
Currey looks like he wishes he was five inches taller and
built wider, built like me. Drugs, I decided, was the sad
story. This was western Massachusetts, remember, where
you get points for being a reformed something. I knew
while I was talking he wasn't seeing this as anything like
pathetic. When he started naming players, and almost
tripped me up on the dates of my tenure, I just nodded
sadly, and made him think all that was so far away I hardly
thought about it anymore. I put on a face. Now I had a wife
and son, I told him, and wanted to do right for them,
wanted to help other troubled kids like the one I'd been
myself. I almost had the teaching certificate, I said. I'd gone
back to school for precisely this reason, and had just one
course left to go. Hearing this last, he looked at me with a
second's doubt, but then the natural envy he felt won over.
He wanted to be close to me, I could see.

After that, Currey took a special interest. When, two or
three months into my employment, my wife kicked me out,
he said he was going to help me land on my feet. He actually said that. I had a girlfriend, though, and I was moving
in with her. There wasn't any problem at all. But Currey
invited me to his house and cooked a barbecue. It was July,
very heavy air and this yard full of vegetables growing. This
was before Currey's wife had been diagnosed. She had a
glow on her, and she wore something green that night. Her
dress looked dark against her skin and against that whitish
blond hair of hers that makes her look like Currey's twin. I

could tell she didn't like looking at me, that I scared her or else my presence here didn't make it the sort of family social evening she enjoyed. She tolerated me is about the best you could say. I didn't help things much by answering her questions with just the single word yes or no. After they put their kids to bed, we all three sat there in the dark of the yard and Currey kept saying, "John's going to be fine," over and over. I knew as soon as I was gone Currey's wife would say, "Don't trust him." No matter. I remember thinking how much I liked sitting there in the cool yard with them, drinking beer and thinking of my girlfriend back at the house, waiting. But in order to have this good moment, I had to pretend I was broken up.

My wife will tell you people like me don't have empathy, but I find I do when I think of Currey and the cancer. Maybe it's a different kind of empathy. I know a lot of people, my parents included, believe that if you do certain things in this life, you are exerting a kind of order, and that such order, if staunchly maintained, will keep certain other things at bay. I'm sure Currey sat on his deck many a night and saw old age coming, could feel the sweetness of all he had to look forward to made solid by the good things with which he'd surrounded himself. He couldn't see, behind the tree, Brother Cancer waiting to steal in. Who could? And I can see now how he must feel cheated, how he must look at those same good things—the trellises and the new deck and the gas grill—with contempt now, how his whole view of the world must be toppling. I can see all that, but there's no way I'd ever call him and say, "Come on, Currey, I'm gonna help you land on your feet." There's a place where empathy stops and presumption starts, and I make sure I never cross that line.

⊠

When I finally get around to calling my girlfriend Cathy, she tells me I can pick her up after work but that I'll have to take her to her doctor's appointment and then wait. It's an appointment she's had for a month, since before I walked into Dr. Petticord's office and took over her life. Well all right, I tell her. At lunch I ask my mother which of their friends are around and which have taken off for Ocean City. I am thinking of the boats docked at the end of our street. She asks me why I want to know and I tell her I might like to take out one of the boats. I used to sail them all when I still lived here. She tells me I shouldn't do anything without permission and I nod, not pressing things.

After lunch I go down to the dock and look at the Heers' and the Coopers' boats, the last two left, and settle on the Heers'. It takes me an hour to find where Ray Heer hides his keys, and by then it's gotten hot, so I take off my shirt and lie down on the dock. It must be that I check out then, because the next thing I remember is opening my eyes to see the sun in a different place, just a few inches above the topmost house on the bay. It's a pretty sight. I stretch up my hands and keep waiting for a sound. There's a car every once in a while, but no kid's cry, no sound of a woman shouting, or a man. Where I grew up, in the house my parents lived in before they built this one, the streets were always full of kids. Now I imagine the kids are all inside, waiting at their TV screens for their mothers to bring them little snacks on a tray. When I think back on my life, it seems to me that a silence came over everything. Maybe it was in the seventies; in any event, there is a definite sense of before and after. Some tide of life receded back then. I felt like I was running with a lot of people and then I was run-

ning alone. My friends, all the boys who fancied themselves
wild, seemed to have gotten scared, and I could not then
understand why. We all had the same kind of parents, big,
dim, and overprivileged. At night our parents got into
cars and drove into Baltimore to see the road company of
Man of La Mancha. That was their idea of a good time.
Afterward, they screwed. We heard them sometimes, heard
our mothers shout things like "Goddamn!" in the night,
and wondered where those women went during the day.
During the day, they played "The Impossible Dream" on
the stereo and dusted. They made these sharp divisions
between things.

My wife used to ask me how I could lie so much. She
said, how can you lie to Currey, how can you tell him you
were a football player when you never were? I told her
there were a lot of reasons and then I just stared at her and I
saw the same fear I used to see in the faces of my friends.
Everybody's afraid of falling through the cracks. Everybody
has their own personal vision of hell, and for a lot of them, I
suspect, it's just an inch or two below the ground they walk
on. So they test each step, and like as not pull back. The
only difference between me and them, I suppose, is that I'm
not afraid of falling. I tend to land on my feet, you see, with
or without Currey's help. I suspect others would, too, more
than wouldn't, anyway, if they let themselves go. But they
don't, they're afraid of knowing that about themselves. So
they stay in their houses, quiet as mice, listening for the
crack. And even for the careful ones, it comes. Currey heard
it, that's for sure. It seems to me that even if you play by the
rules, the same thing happens. We're just fools to believe
otherwise.

At five on the nose, I'm at Dr. Petticord's office, waiting

for Cathy. Then I take her to her appointment, sit in the waiting room thumbing through a copy of *Newsweek*. I read about AIDS and then about some Russian dancers performing in Minneapolis. *Newsweek* thinks these Russians are the cat's meow. There are kids here waiting to see one of the doctors, and their presence makes me think of my son, Will. I used to take him to the doctor's. He was decent company, but I never allowed myself to think about a future together for us, fishing trips and such. I let it be, and that was what made it good. He misses me, I know, but he's got his grandfather. There'll be a man around, at least, to keep him from his angry mother. You came from her, I'll tell him if he ever asks. You came out of her blood and bone and desire. I never had any part of it. I'll be like those black fathers you read about who, when they see the kids they've fathered in the neighborhood, they pass right by them. I just fucked your mother, boy, is what they say.

After Cathy's done, we go to eat at a fish take-out place. Then I bring her down to the Heers' boat. There's no one on the dock and it's almost dark, so it's okay. She asks whose boat this is, and I say people's. We make out a little. She still wants to know. I lay her down on the bed, which forms a *V* from being nestled into the bow. I'm going to have to watch my head here 'cause it's low. It's always very solemn for me, and I study her big eyes in the blue light coming in off the dock. She's got little breasts, but down below there's substance enough to make up for it. I don't like them real skinny, though I do tend to like them small. When I undress I enjoy the way she holds herself back at first. She wants me to make her into what she is. Women like Cathy like to come to that stupid moment in the middle of the act where they half-shout, "I'll do anything

for you, tell me what to do!" They don't understand they've
been doing that from the first.

In a little while, Cathy closes her eyes and goes into that
dreamy place. Her mouth opens. It's nice to watch. All day
long at the therapist's office, she's been waiting for this, and
now I make a present of it. This is our whole agreement,
though we could never say that out loud. Then we lie there,
and she still wants to know whose boat this is. I ask her
what does it matter, and she says she wants to know things
about me, who my friends are and stuff. I say nothing, but I
can feel she's not going to let it go. Does it have to do with
the screenplay? she asks finally, and it makes me laugh to
think what a bad lie this one is. What's so funny? she asks. I
suppose I should be grateful she hasn't gotten to the point
of criticizing my laugh. It's still all part of the one thing.
What I do now is get up and go looking for Ray Heer's
liquor cabinet. When I finally find a half-empty bottle of
Glenfiddich, I pour two tumblers and bring one to Cathy.
This is the weirdest thing, she says. I say, what? That I
don't know anything about you except that you're Dr. Petticord's patient. Well how about I drop out, I say, and then
you won't even know that? She drinks like she's thinking
about it and I listen to the water making its little lapping
sounds against the boat.

She's sat up, though; there's some resistance in her pos-
ture I can see I'm going to have to probe.

Come on back to bed, I say. Come on lie down, Cathy.
She tilts her head so I am looking at her profile, but she
doesn't lie down. She's twenty-four, and she's been waiting
all her life for a man who looks like me to walk through the
door. I say this not out of conceit, but because I look the
way a lot of women imagine their future husbands to look,

tall and regular. Once that man comes into her life, though, it's not a matter for Cathy of simply falling hard; she's too shrewd for that. There are calculations still to be made, expectations to be met, basic standards. These are what absorb her as she offers me her profile. It's not hard to see the life Cathy imagines for herself. At heart, it's no different from the life my friends' mothers had: "The Impossible Dream" on the stereo, dustrag in hand. Only for Cathy it wouldn't be "The Impossible Dream"; something more modern, something to make her feel more in tune with her time. Still, it's what I call the interior life, a life lived inside, within the fortress.

I want to see where you live, she says all of a sudden.

Is it such a big deal? I ask. But I can see right away she's very serious. I try to delay her, but eventually we get dressed and drive up the hill to where my parents' house sits overlooking the Severn.

It's impressive; I suppose that's got to be said, though it's really just a big box with hundreds of windows. The architect's whole idea seemed to be to start with a central ugliness and try to redeem it with light. Nice for him. My parents must have seen it as some grand opportunity to start over, to remove whatever shabbiness once attached to their early, messy romantic lives. Apparently, the ideal is to live out a mature existence surrounded by golf trophies and issues of *Baltimore* magazine.

This is where you live? Cathy asks, impressed. I think up to now she's believed, on the basis of the car I drive, that something would have to be done about the scale of my ambitions.

It's my parents' house, I announce, unembarrassed. I'm staying with them.

The light is on in the big second-floor room, where they

are probably now watching television. The window facing us is wide and broken by thin strips of cedar. The glass is slightly ridged, so that any stray robber would not be able to tell, as Cathy and I are not now strictly able to tell, whether the light signifies the presence of bodies, of life, or merely a light turned on in an empty room. I know their habits, though, so I can easily imagine them sitting there with their evening cognacs, watching one of those TV shows where life seems slowed down to an unbearable degree, and everyone's main business seems to be the thinking up of wry wisecracks.

Are you going to take me in and introduce me? she asks, unable to move her eyes from the place.

This is a bad time, I say to the back of her head. Then I flick on the radio, with the idea that I might distract her. She's turned to me now. I can feel the weight of her focus. Girls like Cathy may not have tremendous intelligence, but the two or three things they do know they carry like bricks behind their eyes. If she meets my parents, she becomes an entity in the house. She gets discussed over the morning eggs. She knows all this, and it gives her a little thrill.

How about tomorrow night? I ask. My mother would love to make you dinner, but she needs some warning. Then I look at her. She's deciding whether to believe me or not. Would you like to see the yard? I ask.

Since the house is built into the side of a hill, there's a delicate ladder of steps we have to descend. At the bottom, my parents' land flattens out for several yards, and they've set up an arrangement of wrought-iron latticework furniture at the very edge, just before the land begins to slope down again toward the river. I sit Cathy down on one of these chairs. There's a fine view of the river, but her eyes are all on the house. She's nervous, I can tell, like maybe

I'm lying about all this and we're going to be caught. I pat
her hand. It's still warm and the soft river scent is intoxi-
cating. Stop looking at the house, I want to say. Instead I
look down through the trees and wait out my time.

It occurs to me as I'm doing so that though this particular
set of furniture has been here as long as I can remember, I
can still count on the fingers of one hand the number of
times I've seen anyone sitting here. It seems another one of
my parents' elaborate arrangements, things set up carefully
and tastefully to accommodate life and then left empty.
Life skirts them somehow, having this tendency to dry up
around good things. I think Currey might agree with me
here. It tends to land elsewhere, in unrulier places.

There was a run I used to take up in Massachusetts, in
the late afternoons. It would lead me past this one house,
big yard, messy as hell, real *Tobacco Road* material. An empty
tractor-trailer sat out in the backyard rusting, and the dog
they kept was always trying to nip at me. One afternoon,
the two kids who lived in the house were out on the older
kid's go-cart, something his father must have patched
together for him. They were going round and round in
circles, the little one in the big one's lap. It struck me that
day that what I was seeing in their faces was the great gift all
the earnest, worried parents like my wife and Currey are
searching for: family happiness, I suppose you'd call it.
Everyone's ideal. My wife was always trying to dress Will
up and put him behind the fanciest, most high-tech toys.
He's a handsome boy, though a little on the pale side, and
he tended to shy away from the robust life. My wife was
always looking at him a little disappointed, like why wasn't
he enjoying all the bounty she offered him, why did he seek
out corners and resist the fancy swing set? Cathy had that
bug, too, I could tell, that lust for the Good Life, the one

that comes ready-made, that we believe we can just step into. She couldn't stop looking at the big wall of the house and thinking we were trespassing. So I got down on my knees before her and tried to distract her. At first she pushed me away, but it must be said Cathy has her sensual appetites, too, and she drew my face up after a while and said, "No, I want something else to go there."

What I was looking for was an act whose elegance might redeem the lawn furniture; well, let's go further, might redeem the whole landscape, bring people out of their houses to watch and stare. What I like about my own body is that it has mass; I'm not one of those little flitting, spoon-chested men you see in bathing suits and wish would put their clothes back on in a hurry: you've got to take me in. So when she took my shirt off, I was glad to have my wide white back exposed. Oh Cathy, I must have said, or some such, being in the early stages of excitement. There's nothing splendid about her, as I said, and when she's naked I don't want to worship her so much as cover her, the way you might want to feed some starving child or bathe some filthy stranger. Oh here, escaped my lips, and I thought of the perfect sense of it, that we were about to do the deed on these *chairs*, and that for just these few minutes Cathy wasn't engaged in some mean calculation as to her own future. Instead, she was welcoming in her sordid present— "Come on in," she was practically saying—some black-haired stranger who for all she knew might end up killing her or leaving her but for now was just doing the one perfect thing. And splendidly, too, I might add, with her head cradled softly in one large hand. She had started, too, her eyes half-closed and her mouth partway opened, when the big searchlight came on and I looked up and saw my father on the rear deck, scowling.

⊠

"That was an asshole thing to try and do" is what my father says after the drinks are poured and we are sitting in the living room. My first impulse is to correct him: I did more than *try*, Dad. He's a tall man who carries himself with a certain grace, but no one in their right mind would ever call him handsome. I get my looks from my mother's side.

My mother is in the kitchen making tea while my father delivers this jeremiad. It's an old story with the three of us, dating back to high school, when I began doing this sort of thing. They made a big fuss when they found us, but it's their sort of fuss, which is not like anyone else's. I told Cathy to go on up to my room and wait this out. Then I watched my father mix the drinks in his slow way, and I swear while he was doing this, he forgot what it was we were supposed to talk about. A son's naked ass exposed to the moonlight, what is that, anyway?

"You're thirty-five years old," he says next. It's an exhaled statement, something he just wants to rid himself of, hardly directed toward me at all. As it happens, he's off by a year, but even I am not smart-ass enough to point out his mistake at this moment. He reaches for his drink and takes some, and I mimic his elegant gesture. I am beginning to feel the bourbon, and it makes me want to talk, but I reason I'd better shut up and endure this. Then I will take Cathy home. We'll stop somewhere and finish what we started, that is if she's not too pissed off at me. So rain down the blows, Daddy. Let them come and let's move on. But there's a silence now. My father rattles the cubes in his glass and looks over my shoulder at my mother in the kitchen. Then his eyes settle back on me and his face takes on this look of distaste.

"Doesn't it *humiliate* you to find yourself in this situation, John?" he asks, and leans forward. "Coming *home* like this, being found . . ." His hand gestures to the vague outdoors, that place into which he's poured so many thousands of dollars yet which he can't imagine any use for, least of all that divine one to which I have so recently put it.

"I don't feel humiliated at all," I answer, and then I just look at him. The two of us share this glazed-eyed stare, neither really focusing on the other, and I suppose the wish on both our parts now is that this were over. He's not really so bad, my old man, just soft and a little past it. ("Ha *ha*," he'll say on the golf course, when someone makes a joke, keeping his eyes open, same as me.)

My mother comes in then, with her tea, and sits on the couch, and makes a great fuss of arranging herself and taking a long, somewhat noisy sip. My father's eyes are all on her, as if at any second she's going to spill something, or else fall. He's that way with her now, all closed in on her, the way a man with an unreliable car might get, listening all the time to its plinks and rattles, so that if you say something to him, he probably won't hear you. And then suddenly he's up, with his hands in his pockets, jingling the coins there, and I'm convinced the worst is over; he's going to bed.

"Your father and I have decided, John"—it's my mother's voice that speaks, though my eyes remain trained on my father; he's the one who seems about to act, but it's a feint, just something to distract me—"that it's not right for you to go on living here with us."

Finally I've got to look at her. She puts her cup down and pats her hair. It's one of those wave jobs hip older women wear now, but it exposes her neck in a way I find unbecoming. It's a good thing to do, though, patting her hair, since it gives her an activity to cover her own awkwardness. I'm admiring the strategy, even as I'm ready to pounce. I don't like to make it easy on them, even when, *especially* when, logic seems to favor them.

"Not right?" is what I ask then, since that's the weak link in her sentence.

"Well . . ." She dusts her lap. It's a neat, small gesture, but it does its work, lets me know it'll be futile to pursue my little trick, that she's said what she's said and, however much I might dig at her weak spot, she retains the power not to let it affect her. "Something like that," she says, and moves her hair, and finally looks up at me. It's a composed look, very even and steady and distant.

I wait for her to break, but she doesn't. Instead, her eyes hold still, and not a little cold. She's good, my mother. She's always been able to hold her ground, when it came to that, and I think everything I've learned in life I've learned from her.

It's really a simple message she's sending me now: It's time for her to be alone, her and my father, time for the two of them to go into the world they've made. It's odd. I'm in the midst of this scene, I'm sitting right across from them, but I'm seeing them on a veranda somewhere, an old missionary couple, maybe, in a photograph. They've sent this postcard to their son, who lives in another country. In the bottom corner is written, in Mom's shaky but still legible hand, "Love, your parents." That's Mom's teaching, right there: not to see people as the helpless and vulnerable creatures they may wish to appear, but as if they exist, at all times, behind the laminated surface of a postcard, lacquered and remote.

"You can take your time, of course," she says. I don't know what I'm looking at now. I shift in my chair. "But not this anymore. Not here. All right?"

She's attempted to be feminine and motherly on that "all right." It's the kind of move you can afford to make only when you know you've already won.

My father is looking down at me. If anything, it's the old man who's feeling guilty about all this, and his concern, which makes his face look droopy and mangy, like an old hound's, makes me laugh. The little hiccup comes out. It's like a small turd someone's left in their living room. They seem to agree, at the same time, not to notice it.

My mother rocks forward onto her knees. It's a first step in the elaborate process of getting up. She has arthritis, and such movements often appear graceless and painful. I don't avert my eyes, though. My father leans forward, accepting her into his arms, and when she's up, in the moment before he lets go, it seems as though the two of them are about to start dancing. They're locked for a moment in that sort of embrace, her head tilted back just a little, his hovering over her, like they're going to dance away from the problem of John. You construct a life, is what their every move has always taught me. You do not live it, not close to the belly, as I have always tried to do; you find the pieces and delicately arrange them so that they form a design, an imitation that will not spoil. And then when the time is right, or else gradually, over time, you rub out what is unpleasant.

My father's arm completes its motion—it's like a small, weird arc in the air—and it breaks the illusion that they're about to go off in their own version of the Anniversary Waltz. Instead, they hover awhile in my presence, not really looking at me but not judging it seemly to move off just yet.

I'm certainly not going to help them out any. My look is as blank as I can make it. Finally they do manage to extricate themselves. There's some business with the dirty teacup in the kitchen. For some reason it takes both of them to get it placed in the dishwasher. My father asks me to shut off all the lights before I come to bed.

A little while later, I realize he hasn't left it up to me, hasn't quite trusted me, because I hear Cathy making her way down the stairs in the dark. By now I've forgotten all about her. She curses, and asks me where the switch is.

Cathy takes on this bandy-legged look sometimes when things haven't been going well for her. Her shoulders get stiff, and she carries them high, so that she resembles Olive Oyl. She doesn't sit beside me, where I've gestured, but across from me, in my mother's place. This, I suppose, is my punishment.

"I've been sitting up there forever," she says, by way of complaint.

"I know."

"So? What happened?"

"We had a small disagreement."

She's aware I'm being coy, but chooses not to push it. It's family business, after all, and she knows better than to intrude. She's checking out the room, besides, which she didn't get to do before, when she was being exiled.

"Did they say anything about me?"

"No. Not a word."

This is a disappointment, I can tell. She's only the bimbo of the evening, in their view. She runs her hands down the sides of her skirt as if she's wiping them clean.

"I want you to tell me the truth about yourself, John."

She turns to me with that wide-open face of hers that makes me remember what it was, when I first walked into

Dr. Petticord's office, that gave me to understand how I could have her very easily. This is not, I realize now, precisely the same thing as having wanted her.

There's all of a sudden a terrible stillness in the room. I recognize this mild urge I have to break something.

"Okay," I answer, and I do, I tell her about my life. As I tell it, I recognize how it sounds unflattering, like a record of drift. Eleven jobs since college, that sort of thing. But I'm also aware that there are two stories going on, the one I'm telling her, which has all the earmarks of "truth," and the one I'm telling myself, which has a fine icebergy consistency to it, and which consists mostly of remembered sensations. In my memory, my life seems to have played itself out almost entirely in a series of afternoons. The light is always the same, and the sensations, which are various, are nearly always centered—again—in my belly. I come to realize something about myself: that I am one of those people— and for all I know there could be millions, this could apply to *everybody*—whose lives have precious little to do with the events that hold them up. Instead, it is as though I found, early, some remote secret place of infinite satisfaction, and chose to live there; chose to call that my life.

I end with the last part, with the job I had up north teaching troubled kids. How I forged the certificate when they demanded it. I am remembering Currey's face as it looked that day he had to fire me, and though there were a great many things mixed there, one of the things I saw was unquestionably desire. It was nothing so simple as homosexual desire; still, it gives me the sense now of possibilities unmet.

As for Cathy, I am watching her the whole time I'm talking. This is not her finest hour. What about the screenplay? she keeps wanting to ask. It's like out of the dregs of all these discouraging facts I'm relating to her, a pure line will emerge. "And then I went to Hollywood and sold a screenplay for a million bucks." That sort of ending. It doesn't come. I finish and then I watch her. I'm waiting. It's her move.

There's a moment—I've been there enough times so I know this—when a woman's looking at you and you come to see in her look your whole future set spinning like a dime on a tabletop. They're deciding. The dime could come up heads or tails. You have no way of knowing, so you hold your breath. Maybe not your whole future, but enough of it. Right now Cathy could solve my problem—where to stay. I'm watching her, and I have this nice detached feeling that her next move is going to tell me something.

I watch her pull a thread on the sofa beside her. She's hesitating, I know, and at this point my heart's racing a little; I'm on tenterhooks to find out what she's going to decide. Her eyes land on Will's picture on top of the TV. He's a fine-looking boy, even with the paleness, the sort of boy every woman wants to have. A future heartbreaker is what they call him. I see the way she looks at him.

And then, focusing on this look of hers as she contemplates my son, I do something that surprises even me. I say, "I'll take you home."

She stares at me, disbelieving. I've rushed things, and she's not happy about it. If she's going to extricate herself from this, she'd rather do it herself, thank you.

But at least there's no fight about it. What leg would she have to stand on, anyway? I've forced the dime to land on tails. I've pressed my thumb down hard, and this feels mildly exhilarating, if only because I've never done it before. Never tried to save anyone from me, or from themselves. I suppose something in that look my mother gave me spooked me a little. I see how willing Cathy might be to want to change me. I believe she'd see that as possible, doable; on some level, they all do, the urge to live this sort of domestic life is that strong. You start out with a lie—that the man is changeable—but you somehow convince yourself it's not a lie, that it's something minor, a thing that will evaporate. And then, what's worse is, you get pregnant. It's a thing that happens. Cathy's twenty-four. I have no doubt in my mind she'd have a kid. And I couldn't tell you right now which would be worse, to abandon him the way I've done with Will, or for the two of us to grow old together like my parents, and to gradually work ourselves to the point where our own son is something we want to refine ourselves out of.

I drive Cathy to Dr. Petticord's parking lot, where her car is. I watch her walk to the car and then fish in her bag for her keys. I can tell it's something she wishes she didn't have to do. The clean getaway is denied her. But I won't be seeing Dr. Petticord anymore. This is the last of our exchanges.

After that I drive around awhile. I've got some things to figure out. They're not so hard, but still I've got to do this. At least I don't feel like making love. The residue of that last unfinished act with Cathy seems to have vanished. Maybe not entirely, but enough so that I'm not bothered by it. It's worse when I get it this time of night and I can't find anyone. Sometimes I drive around for hours.

By the time I get home, I've made a decision. I sit on my bed for a few minutes before I call. Then I pick up the phone and dial Currey.

It's late by now—it's nearly one. I'm expecting to hear Currey's tired voice. I'm going to ask him if I can stay awhile. He'll be surprised, and he'll hesitate. But he wants me in his life; I knew that from the first moment. It's his wife who answers, though. She doesn't sound tired at all. It's like she's been up by herself and she's grateful someone's called. But she talks quickly, in this fierce, urgent whisper, like she doesn't want anyone in the house to know she's up, she's talking on the phone.

"Hello," she says.

I pause. I deal with my surprise.

"It's John," I say. I know she doesn't remember. Who was I, after all? I was there one night, that's all. It's very odd. When I speak again, I hear a whole other thing in my voice. Some edge, some languor. I don't know what you'd call it. It's how you talk when you want someone to remember you, when you want it to be like you're the only, the most important man in the world.

"It's John," I say again. "John from work."

Don't ask me how I know these things, but I do. It's all there in the way she pauses after I say that, in the hush on the phone. I see her in her surroundings, her hair and the nightshirt she's wearing, which would be cotton and reach halfway down her thighs. Outside would be the darkness of the yard, and she'd be looking there, looking at the deck chairs, maybe, or at the skin of a tree. I've got to work hard to see her behind the laminated surface of the postcard, in the grip of the world she's made for herself, the world that little riot of the cells is trying to steal her away from. She doesn't know yet that she's just gotten lucky, because her urge now is to leap out of this closed, perfect world. I try to let her know, with just the deep and subtle sound coming from my throat, that someone's waiting to catch her.

THE CUT OF HIS JIB

When I was fifteen years old, I mowed lawns for the summer. My biggest job (eleven dollars) was the house on the corner of our street. The man was a lawyer; his name was Matt Romano. He might have been thirty-seven then, a lean, tall, handsome man whose good looks—and this was nothing unusual, a characteristic of certain men of the time—bore a faint whiff of the criminal.

No one else on the street was quite like him, though. The men were older, for one thing. My father was older. They were Italian men who had started poor, worked hard, and "risen," so that they'd been able to move from their cramped neighborhoods to this woodsy, "exclusive" hill. Here, they bought half-acre lots and built their big, modern houses, most of them acting as their own contractors. A common style had been agreed to for all the houses: two-story, split-level. The Delosas lived across the street, and the Zagamis. On our side there were us and the Noceras. It was all very serious, living there. You felt, distinctly, your father's pride in having ascended.

The house at the end of the street was vacant for the first few months after we moved in. Deluria, the contractor, had built it on spec, and rumor had it he was asking too much. We, the families, big with our new sense of ourselves as landed gentry, sat around our tables after dinner and discussed such things. The side yard of the vacant house sloped downward, following the curve of the hill. The ledge that had had to be blasted in order to build some of these houses obtruded in spots, with vegetation sprouting from it. The house had, perhaps, more grandeur than the other houses because of this, and because of the number of trees in the back. Amidst them, Deluria had planted a fountain, an angelic woman pouring water from a jug. Couples came on Sundays to look at the house, but none of them seemed quite up to the task of living in it. The Sunday Matt Romano came, the air had a heightened quality; that is the way I remember it, though I know some parts of my memory are the result of additions, things gathered to the central, bare fact because they seem, now, appropriate. We had moved into our house in mid-fall and this was the beginning of spring. Lawns had only just been seeded, so the way I remember it—all the families gathered on green lawns, standing like alerted shepherds to view the coming of the Romanos—cannot be exact. More likely it was me standing alone in my driveway, while a family stepped out of a gold car, a Mercury Cougar, I think. First, a man who looked like he'd just emerged from the cover of a novel, in a blue double-breasted blazer and cream-colored slacks. Then a wife, with honey blond hair and sunglasses, followed by two daughters, dark-haired, like him. They carried about them an air of difference; something made you look at them as if, were you only to stare hard enough, you'd find something out. She was with them that day, I remember that much with absolute assurance. She emerged from the car last, a smaller, darker woman, much younger than his wife but too old to be his daughter. She wore sunglasses as well, but she removed hers. She took them off and glanced across the seeded lawn at us, for only a second's lapse. My father must have come out and joined me by then, because I remember it was the two of us staring at her.

He was, from the beginning, a kind of odd duck. I never heard those words used, but I imagine hearing them used in an overheard conversation, my father and mother talking, my father and one of the men. This is what should have happened. They ought to have stepped back and understood him, dismissed him with one of the functional phrases they had invented for such men. Instead, they did what was natural for them: they accepted him. He became, almost immediately, a part of the crowd. They socialized on Saturday nights, nearly every week, in one or another of the neighbors' basements (but these were not basements, understand; they were "lower levels," carpeted, with big pool tables and pine paneling). My father's idea of a good time was to gather all the men into his office as soon as they arrived and ask them to take off their clothes and get into women's dresses and wigs. Then the men, dressed as women, would come out and dance for their wives, the "girls," who would sit together on couches and giggle uproariously. From our rooms upstairs, my sisters and I would hear them and sometimes creep to the banister and watch these hairy, half-exposed men in scanty costumes, from the bottom of which their boxer shorts showed. In dresses and wigs, they looked more like men than they would have in their regular party clothes. That was the nature of the game; I understood, early on, that it was all about sexual display.

My father loved to tell the story of the first time Matt Romano came to one of these parties. He grabbed him by the arm, took him into his office, and said, "Take off your pants." "You should have seen his face!" My father laughed. He is a simple man, my father; when he laughs, his face goes red. He believes deeply, I think, that every man is at heart the same man, with the same desires, save for those few who are so perverse that they must be set aside from the rest. "And then," my father went on, "in the next minute, he did it!" It was Matt Romano's initiation as ordinary man. He removed his blue double-breasted blazer and the cream-colored slacks and put on a dress and a wig. I did not watch this particular party, but I saw other scenes enough like it so that I can imagine how Matt Romano would have arranged his face into a pose of easy mirth, so much like the others that anyone would have been fooled. Then he would have gone out and bared his legs, and the men would have laughed, very hard, and put their hands on his shoulders, and laughed again.

Very soon, his name began to change. I had thought, on first hearing it, that it had a certain elegance that put him at a distance from the others. And they spoke it, too, that way at first, with a kind of perplexed respect. Who was this man, this newcomer, this lawyer who had moved in among them? His practice was in Boston. Much was made of that, his city life, his professional life, his physical removal from the cement trucks and Laundromats and muddy construction sites of my father and his cronies. It is easy enough to imagine him as he might have existed in those days, in his office with its view of the harbor. In my image, he is speaking on the phone, leaning forward, scratching the side of his nose, a familiar habit of his. Several stories below, the water runs slate gray, smoky in the afternoon light. Yet I can't hold the image without seeing him turn away from the things on his desk, the crisp papers, the letter opener. He looks down and away, riveted by something. There in the harbor, my father and Steve Delosa are out on my father's Chris-Craft, fishing for flounder off of Rainsford Island. They are wearing fishing jackets, funny hats; in their hands are cans of beer. He is staring at them intently; there is something he is trying to figure out, a desire he is probing. Already, they have put a spin on his name, something that does not displease him. In their flat Boston pitch they stress the *an* in Rom*an*o. All its languor, its otherworldliness, is being ironed out. They are making him, in all the ways they know how to, just like them.

There is only the fact of Sundays to stand in the way of this ongoing absorption: on Sundays she comes, the slender, dark-haired girl in sunglasses. She wears dresses that cling to her small body, and she moves with the cautious precision of someone crippled in youth. Very soon, it seems, everyone knows her name. "Did Dolores visit the Romanos today?" my mother might ask my father on a Sunday evening, as if she hadn't herself looked and seen. And the name will not be reduced, not the way they have reduced his name. The word *Dolores* cannot be bitten down on; it comes out, in spite of their best attempts, sounding ambiguous, dreamlike, a word from another place, one they have steadfastly determined not to visit.

Dolores was Matt Romano's secretary. That explanation arrived a month or so after the Romanos moved in. I don't know when the neighbors had begun to wonder about their Sunday arrangement, but I know the explanation, the business relationship, was spoken of with relief. After that, all forms of apocrypha sprang up. She was an orphaned girl for whom the Romanos had agreed to stand as substitute family. Her relations lived far away, in "California." The weekends were hard for her. She had nowhere else to go.

A snapshot: it is early summer, before Matt Romano has asked me to start mowing his lawn. I am in my backyard. I do not know what I am doing. Perhaps when you are fifteen, you only watch; it is your principal task, whatever other functions your body might be performing. It is your obsession to figure out the world. Matt Romano and Dolores are alone in the backyard, and from two houses away I can see them. They are walking among the trees in the Romanos' backyard, the miniature forest of tall maples. Her dress is blue and belted; she is wearing a straw hat. He is walking slightly ahead of her and gesturing. His long arm goes out, as if to make a point; he turns to her. For a moment he considers her the way I was later to see him consider many things, as if from a far remove, something passing briefly over his face that to an outsider might resemble contempt. Then something else. The afternoon, for two or three seconds only, is heavy with an essence that I know, even at fifteen, he believes to be at the heart of life. If I had now to put a name on that thing I was made aware of, I would fumble, I would choose a useless word like *confusion*. Like *ambivalence*. But at that instant, as I stand in the presence of it, I seem to understand that there is no need to name it. It is simply there, on Matt Romano's face as I view it from a distance, a seeing into life that troubles him deeply, yet that he is brave enough to hold on to for these few seconds. Then he moves past it—his body does, anyway; they sit on the edge of the fountain and resume their conversation. He goes on gesturing with his arms. Dolores sits upright, listening attentively but at the same time with an air of distraction, as though the important thing was said a while ago, and she is struggling to absorb it while only pretending to hear the words he is saying now. Through all of this, I have remained unseen.

In July, at someone's cookout, he spoke to me for the first time.

"I hear you're a pretty good lawn mower," he said.

I don't remember answering. It was a bit of a surprise to come face to face with the fact that we inhabited the same universe, that he existed in dimensions identical to mine, was capable of taking me in, even of making a request. But some arrangement must have been made that afternoon, because I began mowing their lawn on Wednesdays. He had offered eleven dollars. The figure was irresistible; his largesse, everything that was impressive about him, was in it. His lawn took half a day. He was at work while I did it. I was fastidious, careful with things like edges and rocks, and I lost myself, always, in the rhythm of the humming machine. Every once in a while I would gaze up at the house, trying to get a closer look. A cedar deck rose on stilts at the far end. Through the window, I could see the cathedral ceiling, the hanging chandelier that would have lit their living room. His daughters were not girls who often played outside, but occasionally the younger one—she must have been five or six at the time—would come out and talk to me. I wanted to say nothing that would offend her, nothing she could report to her father that might cause me to lose this job, so we had a series of careful conversations in which most of our time was spent merely staring at one another. When the mowing was done, I trimmed the borders with clippers and went over the whole lawn carefully to check for any spots I'd missed. After the first time, I made the mistake of going up to the back door and standing before Stella Romano, too embarrassed to ask for money but assuming she would know what I was there for.

At first, she looked at me, then past me, as if I'd come to tell her about some problem with the lawn. And it was as though this worried her: the lawn wasn't her domain.

"I'm finished," I said.

She looked at me again, still not comprehending. Then she finally seemed to get it and laughed in her light, dismissive way. It was mid-afternoon, but she wore a dress, and jewelry. Beyond her, the little girls watched TV in the den.

"You'll have to come back tonight," she said.

I came back after I saw his car in the driveway, and that was the ritual I followed all summer. I left an hour for their dinner, which was later than ours, so that by the time I crossed the two yards I had to leave the very comfortable scene of our house at dusk, the television on in our family room and the yellow evening light coming in, while my sisters painted their nails and my mother did the dishes. My father, his gaze fixed absently on the screen, had set this time aside for what remained of his dream life. I looked forward to the moment when I had some excuse to leave them, to cross the two lawns in the deepening light. Something in that family room at that hour gave me cause to fear. I never probed it, or never far; something was stopped there, something had achieved perfection. I felt oddly freed by the feeling of unsettledness I had as I climbed the steps to the back landing of the Romanos'.

There, the scene was always repeated, always the same— Matt Romano would answer the door and look at me as if he had never seen me before and had no idea what I was there for. Seconds would pass; he would focus, then seem displeased by the fact that had finally risen into his consciousness. I was the boy who mowed their lawn, the neighbor's son come looking for money. He seemed, in his half-unbuttoned white shirt and black dress pants, to have emerged recently from a scene of violence. There was about him an agitation that made me think at any second a wild gesture might spring forth, though he would only reach into his pocket and count out eleven dollars, and as he spoke, in the transparent effort he made to be kind, I came to know that he was only drunk. Behind him, there might have been some noise, a woman's whimpering, though I am quite sure I am reading this in. The single instance Stella Romano appeared behind him, it was the cagey, frightened look of a keeper that she wore; she drew him back when he began to speak to me. His words were slurred; I doubt I even heard him. She must have been afraid, though, of what he might say. She drew him back with one hand, and as I turned to her I lost the haunted look in his eyes, the look that drunks get when they want, terribly, to be understood. There seemed to be in it some message meant directly for me. But it, too, was lost. One or the other of them shut the door.

⊠

It doesn't seem at all strange to me how little my life that summer had to do with the outside world, the world of my peers, how fully and simply I inhabited that neighborhood. I don't think my evening bike rides ever took me beyond the street, or the sand pits that announced foundations that would soon be built on the newly cleared lots opening into the forest. I circled the houses and studied hard, noticed small architectural flaws—the Zagamis had left too much foundation showing, so had my father—and grew attuned to an unnameable melancholy that settled over me as I stared at new brick and stone at dusk. Sometimes I wandered through the skeletons of houses that were still just wood, naming the rooms. If I saw a man walking past— Steve Delosa with his dog, Al Zagami whistling—I would stare hard at that, too, waiting for the image to reveal its deeper truth. The intuition that guided my days was that something was about to be shown to me, some fact about life I had to be alert for, a thing that might free me from what, even then, I could see was not a usual infatuation.

In September, they decided to throw themselves a ball. It did not seem extraordinary, though a far cry from the parties where the men dressed as women. The women were to purchase gowns; the men, tuxedos. I don't think the ball was the Romanos' idea exactly, but I believe it was because of the Romanos that a change occurred. Within a year, the raucous Saturday night cross-dressing became a thing of the past.

There was a school dance that Saturday night, but I didn't go. Instead, I sat in my house and waited for my parents to appear, dressed for the occasion. The Noceras joined my parents for a pre-ball drink, but there was tension as soon as they came in. Elena Nocera seemed uncomfortable, as if waiting to be sprung from the tight white gown she wore, to put her feet up and make one of the ribald comments that were her trademark. Charlie Nocera, too, looked fidgety in his tuxedo. But my father moved about the rooms, appearing purposefully stiff, as though guided by the stately measures of a piece of music none of the rest of us could hear. "Have a brandy, Charlie?" he asked, and went to pour it. Charlie Nocera put his hands in his pockets. Elena made a joke. My mother, in her yellow gown, sat as if in a trance.

When they had all gone into the Romanos', I stood at the foot of their lawn to see what I could of the party. A bay window, twelve feet across, cast its light onto the lawn. A single birch rose up in front, stark and long-trunked. Through its leaves, I watched the pastel women pass, the men in black suits. Matt himself came for a moment and stood at the window. I don't believe he saw me. One hand was in the pocket of his tuxedo pants, the other held a long-stemmed drink. On his face was that by now familiar, wistful suggestion that what was most dear to him, most essential, existed elsewhere. I was sure he was going to step away, come outside, drive off. Around his body was that slight, subliminal blurring, as in a film, where you know an action is forthcoming, and I understood it was the action I'd been waiting for. I might have been coaxing him, hoping for the gesture, the tug of the rope with which all the scenery might be lifted and the mechanics of this world revealed to me so that I might see it, at last, for the blunt thing it was. But all he did was turn away. He went back to the party. The movement of the room seemed to slow down and gather around him, as if he had gotten lost on an outing, stopped somewhere to get a closer look at some amazing, briefly glimpsed thing, and now the others had formed a party to carry him away from it.

I am sorry to say that after that night, or soon after, I began to change. A new school year had begun, different from the one before; circumstances converged in a way that made me grow more interested in myself, less so in the world around me. I lost the perfect outward attunement of a fifteen-year-old boy, and never again recovered it. Or let me say, instead, that I found it, or had it thrust on me, on only two other occasions, so that what might have been a rich, dark, satisfying story becomes instead jagged, a thing of snapshots.

The first occurred at another cookout, during another summer, and it was the only time I saw Matt Romano flare up, openly declare his independence from the others, though when I say "flare up," that's too much; it was subtler than that. The Noceras had built a pool; there were gatherings on Sundays, celebrations, really, of Charlie Nocera's deepening success in the construction business. No one else had a pool. Charlie Nocera's grin grew foxier, wider in those days. You see this gathering of energy in certain men, the moment when they peak. The children are still young, the pool is new, all the calls are for them. He began to take some of the limelight away from Matt Romano. Perhaps Matt sensed this and was annoyed; perhaps that's the explanation for his behavior that day. I don't know. We all leaped into the pool, one nearly on top of the other, but after a time I sat in a lounge chair, wrapped in a towel, taking time off from my growing fascination with myself to pay attention to the men.

They were talking: Matt Romano, my father, Charlie

Nocera, Steve Delosa. The women were elsewhere and the chatter was aggressive, punctuated by laughter, then softening, drifting, falling back into the rhythms of the summer afternoon. Matt Romano began a story. It always surprised me to hear him talk. Whenever he opened his mouth and spoke, I was made certain that I had invented him, invented, at least, the dreaming, wraith-like figure who hovered over the neighborhood but was never quite one with it. When he spoke, he was a coarse man whose eyes revealed the desperation of someone wanting merely to be liked. I turned away. I remember, though, when he'd finished, registering on some level that his story had failed to make the desired impression. The men seemed disturbed by it. Matt had told a story about a rascal, a business cheat he half-admired. The story ended, the men made a kind of silent grumble, then Matt said, in afterthought, "I liked the cut of his jib."

I turned back then, I had to, because some sixth sense told me I was about to witness a scene. Charlie Nocera was sitting, his hands folded, leaning slightly forward, with his thumbs flicking at one another. He was grinning, but the grin had passed its point of animation and some darker assessment was taking place in his eyes. Hatred would be too strong a word for it, but it was not impossible to imagine, from that look, that in other circumstances he might be about to get up and hit Matt Romano. My father leaned back in his chair with one finger pressing against the side of his lips—his thoughtful, impatient pose. Steve Delosa glanced off at the neighboring trees, waiting for something to pass.

All of this took place in a matter of seconds, and within it, I saw Matt Romano watch them all, quietly defiant. "The cut of his jib." It was not language any of them would ever have used; he had brought it from somewhere else and held it before them like a sign of his dual citizenship, his ability to escape their little world, if it came to that. They all knew this: they were antagonists at heart. All their silent acceptance of Dolores, of his transgression of the rules, felt about to erupt. Instead, the unexpected, habitual thing happened. It was as though a bird, emerging from its egg, went backward, covered itself over, so that the egg, though newly whole, revealed its network of cracks. Someone said something, to offset the tension. Matt Romano's face turned grim. Whatever he was seeking took its form in the space between him and the men. He considered it, then lowered his eyes. He leaned back in his chair and crossed his legs. From a distance, it might have appeared as though an ease had returned to the scene. A breeze made the tops of the trees move. Elena Nocera, grinning widely, came out with iced tea.

Finally, we are all on the water, in my father's boat. It is a twenty-seven-foot cabin cruiser, docked in Gloucester. The family sleeps on it Saturday nights in summer; on Sundays the neighbors come. Before noon, they emerge at the top of the ramp, holding coolers, picnic baskets. But now I am no longer interested in them. It is two summers later, 1967; they have gone from being gods to becoming jokes. Not their fault, entirely, or mine. Even beyond my seventeen-year-old consciousness, a passage was going on. They were all suburban Democrats in Ban-Lon pants, and they were being moved, ungently, from the center of the visible universe to some laughable periphery.

Still, they acted as though they hardly knew this. On

Sundays they cooked steaks and drank beer and appeared to me on the other side of the smoke from the grill, men whose clothes no longer fit so well, women outliving their usefulness. My invisibility, once so precious to me, seemed another count against them. I could not understand how they remained so fascinated by themselves and each other. I felt they should turn to me, and stare, perhaps ask a question about the life I was about to go off and seize.

In one of the home movies of his later years, my father did something private, for himself. I came upon it once by accident, looking for something else. On a day when they must have been alone together on the boat, he filmed my mother. She is not doing anything dramatic or particularly interesting. For long stretches, she eats, she puts on sunglasses, she sits staring upward at the sun. She faces him and speaks. There is no sound to the film, so there is only her mouth moving, and the sight of her body, in a one-piece bathing suit. The light is overbright, the water an impossible blue. He holds the camera a long time on her, as though not willing to turn away.

But that was later, all my understanding came later. That day in 1967 I was entirely blind to it. Dolores was still there among them. She might have been thirty then. If there had been delicacy and ripeness to her at the beginning, it was starting to go. Her belly fell into tight ridges that clung to her ribs when she sat. Though she didn't speak often, her voice, when she did, no longer sounded hopeful and tentative and waiting to hear the great defining thing. She was like someone's niece who ought to have been at another party, one with young lawyers and daiquiris, but no one had the grace to tell her so. It had to come through an action.

It was a big party that day: us, the Noceras, the Delosas,

Matt Romano, Stella and Dolores. Six children altogether. It was my job to steer, which I didn't mind doing. I kept a transistor radio at the helm: Top 40 blocked them out. They sat in deck chairs; the women put on kerchiefs to keep their hair from blowing in their faces.

We made a wide circle of the harbor, then edged under the narrow bridge into the Annisquam River toward Wingaersheek Beach. For the most part, that day would have been a day like any other. We always anchored the boat along the mile-long tongue of white sand that stretches from the mouth of Wingaersheek. The dinghy we carried on our stern would have brought the women in to shore. Then, laughter as they tried to go from dinghy to sand without getting wet, and my father, on the outboard motor, would have made a joke, and shaken the boat, to make them nervous.

The men usually chose to swim in, to make big awkward dives and thrash through the water, then emerge, sleek-headed and dripping, before a dry, fully clothed woman. Then the women would have stripped down to their bathing suits, blankets would have been laid out, cigarettes lit.

The only awkwardness—too familiar now for anyone to pay much attention—would have been Matt Romano's emergence from the sea. Dolores stood waiting. She watched him swim in, always, as if at any moment he might be lost forever. Stella would not be so overt: she'd busy herself with the children, the two dark-haired girls. Age had made them lithe, more physical, and Stella was awkward as she ran after them. Little attention as I paid (I stayed on the boat, with one of my sisters; we read paperbacks), I can see the choice as it might have appeared to him that day. Stella, who had put on weight, who rarely in those days allowed herself to be seen in a bathing suit. A yellow or pale green dress flapping against her white legs, the jewelry she was never without—necklace, rings—making a sparkle in the sun. Her hair would fly backward in the wind, her profile standing out, unadorned. Then Dolores, at a distance, arms crossed, a bit impatient. Still, nothing attached to her, no children; she was merely what she was, a woman who had waited a long time for him to make up his mind. One of the men might have come up to her and made a joke—"Look, he's not as quick as he used to be!"—and then she would have laughed edgily and looked at Matt Romano splashing through the sea until some presentiment of the hugeness of her risk made her shiver. Seeing this, his mind would be made up for him, at least for the moment, and he'd go to her, to reassure.

Out of the corner of her eye, Stella would catch sight of this and pretend not to notice. As practiced at acceptance as the neighbors had become by then, there had to be a moment—very brief, a hairline fracture—when the facade began to crack. Steve Delosa would put out a cigarette, with disgust, in the sand. Everyone would know what he meant, awareness traveling like a shared tremor among them. Matt Romano would register it.

But after a while things would slacken, the rhythms of the afternoon would take hold. Cigarettes would be smoked, conversational topics broached. What might have compelled them in the summer of 1967? The advent of the hippies in San Francisco? Lyndon Johnson's escalation of the Vietnam War? A sale at Penney's? The words would have floated on the air, the way they do on a beach, important for a moment, then gone. Elena Nocera would have lain back and made a joke about her legs. One of the men would have adjusted his bathing suit to free his balls. They'd've watched the younger couples as they strolled this length of sand, or made note of the other vessels, or turned in the opposite direction from shore, where the dune grass glistened in the white heat.

It would have been that kind of afternoon. Insignificant. The sun would have gradually lowered in the sky, and it would have been lost, a day gone. Half a mile distant, blankets would have been gathered off the crowded beach, the small exodus to cars begun, thoughts returning to Monday, to the question and the problem of work. For them merely a reflex, that, and then a deeper sinking into the day, the stretching out of legs. What anxiety did "work" have for any of them? Headaches, yes. Problems with suppliers, arguments, but all this would come and go, it was tomorrow's business. They were lucky, and they knew it. They had survived to this point in their lives, rich enough, without encountering any of the stickier problems—all but the Romanos, that is. Tonight the men would make love to their wives the way older men do in summer, when the rising of the skin seems to have less to do with a particular woman than with the quality of the day, and you try to get to it in the last light, when the vestiges of some old existence, one you perhaps never actually lived, are to be found in the edges and crannies of the act itself. On the beach the men would have thought of all that, and the group stayed later than anyone else.

By the time they finally gathered their things, the water would have darkened, fishing boats coming in with their entourage of gulls, and their bodies would have gone heavy, resistant to the transition back to boat, to car. My father pulled the dinghy, loaded with women, through the shallows until the water reached midway up his thighs, then he heaved himself onboard. Another joke, more laughter, his head with its gray nest of hair and then his body, as he half-stood to jerk the motor into life, flinging toward me the brief, unwelcome awareness that he was still vital, still fucked my mother, a terrible thing to know but something he was resplendent with as he pointed the dinghy toward the boat, where I waited with my sister and our novels. The women's faces on the dinghy, the sun behind them, were red, their hair lightened by the salt, and their bodies had the soft-shoulderedness of women who had recently been pleasured. It was as if my father were riding his harem across this weedy patch of sea, a harem of contented, middle-aged women.

Only one thing was interesting that day: Dolores, among them, on the dinghy, and I don't think I'd even remember how she looked if it wasn't the last time I was to see her. Straight-backed with resistance, she sat in sunglasses, her proud little body thinner than anyone else's. She would not give herself over to the happy ease of that boat; if once she'd felt close enough to them to joke, to share secrets, those days were over. She had grown careful to mark out her boundaries and to move within them with precision, so that while the thighs of Mary Delosa and my mother might have been touching, their sweatshirted shoulders blurred and indistinguishable, you saw all the space around Dolores.

They came to the boat and unloaded, my father made playful little grabs for their calves, and immediately they busied themselves, putting away blankets, getting out robes to welcome their children, who were still onshore with the men. None of them watched what was going on there, not at the beginning.

My father had returned to shore and was in the process of getting each of the children loaded into the boat, outfitting them first with life preservers. There was just room, with children on their laps, for the three men as well, though it made the boat ride low. After lifting his daughters in, Matt Romano put up his hand in a gesture of refusal. My father made an answering gesture, beckoning him in. These were repeated, until Matt Romano stepped away from the boat. My father looked at him a moment, unmoving, with just the focus of the others on the boat to tell me he was saying something. Matt Romano lowered his hands into the water, and my father started up the motor. Someone, one of the women, said, "He's going to swim," and then another— not Stella, not Dolores—said, unworried, factual, "It's too far."

The tide had come in enough so that the distance was, in fact, significant. I didn't doubt, though, that he would make it. He was no more than forty then and had a strong body. He moved out to where the water was waist-deep and watched the progress of the dinghy until my father had reached us and we all had begun helping the children onboard. Only when everyone was recovered did he begin his swim, and I was prescient enough even then to understand that, for some reason, he wanted us to watch him.

My father was still standing on the dinghy, but after Matt Romano had swum twenty or thirty feet he decided there was no reason not to lift it and hook it to the back of the boat. As he did so, a look passed over his face, an annoyed look. Charlie Nocera had come and stood beside me to watch his neighbor swim. I could feel the tension of his body even a foot away, and it wasn't an ordinary tension. Something was happening. It could have been the most commonplace of things—a man swimming a long distance—or it could have turned into something else. Charlie and my father didn't know yet. That there was something remarkable about Matt Romano—his occasional, yet highly dramatic, insistence that life could be lived differently than they lived it—was the grit of sand under their suits, the thing they would remove if they could. Yet it was elusive, it might not be at all what they thought it was, so they were denied the clean action that would stop him in his tracks. They could only wait and see.

So he swam, and we watched him, the black knot of his hair dipping, then rising, his Indian's beak of a nose coming up, his wide back glistening in the sun, until someone started to notice what was happening.

It was barely detectable at first. He was veering off course, but just slightly, and it could have been no more than a trick of light that he appeared to be making no progress toward us. We were so taken in by his impressive swimming that it didn't seem quite possible that another force—an invisible one—might be rendering all that beautiful effort in vain. "The current's taking him," one of the men said, finally. He began to slow down after a while and then you could see it more clearly, how it was pulling him, the late-afternoon tug of the tide, so strong on that part of the river. He must have been fifty feet upriver of us when he lifted his head.

She was beside me then, nestled between me and Charlie Nocera but not aware of either of us. She had come to the railing to look, and still there was that space around her, as if she believed this display was for her alone.

It had that quality to it, his moment of failure, because I believed the same thing, that it was for me. His head was lifted now and he was looking at us as though not yet willing to ask for help. Instead, he seemed deliberately to choose this moment, to hold it still and out of time, as a kind of invitation to all of us to see him for what he was; to be accepted for all that he could not quite do.

We all took it in; there was a silence on the boat. I was disappointed, above all other things. I had needed, very badly, to see him as someone capable of breaking free of this world, if he only chose, but now, as I watched him, watched his face, which made no effort to excuse his moment of shame, I saw that he had been caught by it, was, in fact, the same as them, in love with something closer to death than to life. Finally, he let the current carry him up the river until it deposited him on the shore.

As we watched this, I felt the movement of Dolores's body in front of me. She'd gone very close to the railing. Now her shoulders lowered, and the bumps of the vertebrae along her back receded. It was enough to let me know something. My father let the dinghy into the water again; his expression was more satisfied now. The rest of us watched to make sure Matt Romano made it to shore, and then my father, floating, asked, "Anybody want to come for a ride?"

As it turned out, both of the other men wanted to come with him. Matt had been carried far upriver, so as they steered toward him they made a diagonal into the sun. I remember their rounded, coarse backs on the boat. I remember, too, how it occurred to me that, for them, this was not entirely unexpected, this turn of events, that all along they had known what would have to happen to him, and had treated him more or less like a child who would, in time, understand. Only I had been fooled into believing there was, for him, some possibility of escape.

It took twenty years before the life he gave himself over to that day finally killed him. Heart trouble had apparently started much earlier, but more than for most men, the passage from age fifty to sixty had a wasting effect. My wife and I went to visit him and Stella when we were newly married; they had dogs then. We were big with our romance, and all I remember my wife and me doing was talking about ourselves, giving details of our domestic arrangements, our studio apartment in New York, places we had traveled and were going to travel. He listened, and at one point I thought I saw the old contemptuous look come over his face. It was just after Christmas, and he lifted one of the opened boxes in their living room. I leaned forward, relieved, thinking he was going to show me one of his gifts, when suddenly, and with majestic fierceness, he used it to sidearm one of the dogs.

That's all much later; I'm getting ahead. But there wasn't a lot left to that day really. Memory closes down on it, as if it wants to see the end there. He's onshore, waiting for them, his hands on his hips. He doesn't look embarrassed. He's standing straight, merely waiting. Maybe he's calmer now. Something has been settled on, after a long effort. They come in close, the three men, and move over for him, and he steps in and settles among them on the boat, and the four of them ride toward us, black, faceless figures with the sun behind them, and when I look again, she is not there anymore. Without my quite knowing it, Dolores has slipped from her position before me, so that as the dinghy comes very near, I feel a shiver of apprehension that there is no longer anything standing between me and him.

THE SECRET LIFE

I

The summer after their second child was born—a boy!—the Augartens found themselves suddenly and—to Theo, anyway—suspiciously popular. Invitations arrived from the Thalers, the Nagles, the Wohls: the cream of society such as existed in their town. "Congratulations on your new baby" would be scribbled somewhere on the cards. They had known these people lightly, marginally before. "What have we done that all of a sudden makes them want us around?" Theo wondered aloud. "All we did was screw without protection." There were usually a dozen couples at these parties; new decks and porches were lit by citronella candles while, in the backyards, colored lanterns hung from the trees. The scene was arcadian, lush; children playing games at the edge of the light, the Augartens' shy daughter among them. Previously they had driven past such parties, viewed them from a distance, while their daughter, Leah, sat silent in the backseat, clutching a book. For the child's sake alone, the invitations were a blessing. And who was he kidding? For his, too. But it was awkward: during the winter, in the middle of Anna's pregnancy, he had begun an affair—a woman his age, a foolish woman; still, it persisted, and would not go away.

Someone, a friend, had once assured him that every married man had a secret life. This was in the early days of his marriage, when he still clung to his male friends. Now he looked around at the men at these parties and doubted the truth of it. There was something wonderful about these lawyers and therapists and anesthesiologists—big-headed, curly-bearded Jews like himself, mostly, but with chests that thrust outward and heavy, ringing, expansive laughs. They gave in to life; they made a deal and kept it. And he, what did he do? For years he'd denied his wife the second child, this sweet Jacob, sleeping in the Snugli. Not that she'd begged. But caution had been his watchword. Alone, he communed with a second, private self he hoarded and refused to submit to the light. Give completely in to life, and what happened to that precious part of you? It was too much to believe all these others felt the same way. What would happen if he were to shout, as he sometimes wanted to, "I sleep with another woman! Three times a week I plunge into her soft wetness"? Would all the men simply nod and say, "So do we!" and would they then move on to a discussion of the upcoming School Committee election? No, it would mean exclusion for sure. And though that was what he felt anyway, he held back. For his daughter's sake, his wife's. He drank and talked and carried on like everyone else.

Theo was an administrator. A Ph.D. in American history, he worked in the office of an HMO serving three counties. He'd come out of school at a time when the demand for historians was low. Now it was better, but he was ensconced, earning a big salary. At night he read history and lapsed—if it was late, if he was alone—into reveries where he engaged in conversation with those high-born architects of the postwar world he so admired. He imagined drinking with Dean Acheson. "And what's your advice, Theo, should it come to pass . . ." Then he would rouse himself and go and check the doors to be sure they were locked. Sometimes, with the others sleeping, haunted by sudden fears of conflagration, he'd test the smoke alarms, press the lever that forced them to emit a high beep. He always laughed, ruefully: that's my soul talking, that beep.

Anna, his wife, had her own business, breads and desserts that sold briskly in local delis. She worked at home, in the big kitchen, with a special permit and a part-time staff of two. Sometimes he'd surprise her in the middle of the day, find her with sweat on her high forehead and a soiled apron. "Get out of here! Don't look at me like this!" she'd shout, her voice sounding like she'd only left Brooklyn the week before. What he couldn't tell her—there were usually others around—was that he wanted to lift the apron and have her against the counter. Her breasts, unsupported beneath the sweatshirt she wore, looked rounder, and the smell of dough and cornmeal was an intoxicant. She'd been a dessert chef when they'd met, he a graduate student working as a busboy in the same restaurant. At night when the place closed, the staff would gather at the bar, drink shots of Sambuca. She led the drinking, a big, self-confident Italian girl, large hands and feet, wide hips and a red gash of a mouth: could he have her? A lowly busboy, he hesitated at first to approach. But she laughed at his jokes. One night in February, they parked on a cold hill. He prayed for help from someone. God. He wasn't at all certain he could manage it with a woman so seemingly sure of herself. Afterward, there was light from the streetlamp and he studied her face hard. Who was she, really? She'd turned a degree from Barnard into a $150-a-week job making glacéed pears. She was afraid to live too far away from home, a huge Italian family, all girls. She squeezed his big shoulders and took him to her house. "I've always gotten along good with the Jews," her father announced. Even now, at parties, she considered it no insult to her integrity to describe herself as mostly his wife. "Anna," he'd interrupt, "you have your own *bus*iness." "What do I do? I make cream puffs." She was like a boy then, a tough waterfront thug. Anyone looking at him looking at her would read adoration.

But if that were so, why was he spending three afternoons a week in the bed of a spindly blond woman whom he did not care for, a woman with no furniture; a woman whose life, when he looked up from the bed at her surroundings, seemed like it could be wiped off the face of the earth with the flick of a dustrag?

There was no easy and obvious causality; as a former historian, he rejected it. Tremors started deep in the earth, but people were always examining their own piddling actions for points of origination. "It's because I am really *two*," he would say to himself, whenever the question of cause came up, and though this was not a terribly satisfying answer, it was as far as he could get.

The affair—if you could call it that—had begun in the midst of a wet, slushy January. A sudden thaw had filled the streets with puddles, and the sky was perpetually low; in such weather, everyone looks for something. Their offices were on opposite sides of a partition, easy enough to develop a sensitivity to one another's moods. One day, the woman was feeling low, in the midst of a third divorce; kind Theo suggested a drink. They chose a working-class bar, with the television running. In business suits, they looked out of place, but Theo liked these surroundings, an escape from the usual. At the beginning, he drank martinis with too much vermouth in them. "Order Bombay," she suggested, worldly-wise, "and tell them to make it dry." He had the sense that the air of stopped life that existed in this bar was the result of something very dramatic that had recently happened, from which the waitresses and patrons were all recovering. Over drinks, the woman told stories of her last marriage. He nodded his head, sympathetic but cautious. It was amazing to believe this woman had endured what she claimed to have endured. If these stories were all true, why didn't she break?

It became at first a weekly, then a twice-weekly occurrence, drinking in this roadhouse, among couples who drank and didn't speak and looked perpetually exhausted, the women especially. Next to this, his own homelife seemed bright and sparkling and clean, a beacon. This began to have all the feeling of an affair, with none of the mess. Often in his imagination he felt the impulse to crush the woman's shoulders in a thick embrace, to test her softness and her give, but he only did this in his mind, and congratulated himself that there was no need to do it in reality. He loved Anna. And then once, in the parking lot, the woman burst into tears, apropos of nothing—they had been saying good-bye to one another, making a silly joke, and tears had sprung to her eyes. He hugged her. It had begun to snow, a swirling mass in the air. He seemed so big, so large to himself. This was nothing, he thought, to hug a woman.

But after a time, it became impossible to think of anything else. Nothing would have been easier, or more desirable, than to take her in his arms again, but no chances came his way. He was certain she had no interest in him except as a receptacle for stories of the three thugs she had married. At times, it became difficult to keep his hands closed around the stem of his martini glass, or to prevent himself from looking at her in a manner that would give away his growing sense of agitation. Even after he left her, her presence remained with him, rode beside him as he drove home in the car, became his companion as he stayed up reading; he thought of it as a hot line of some substance resembling mercury running from just below his throat down to where he ended. "It's just desire, that's all," he said to himself, and when he said it, said the word *desire*, it seemed a small thing, something he could be expected to manage. Too often, though, the rest of his life was conducted like a thing he wished to rush through, the quicker to land once again in the brown, cracked leather seats of the 999 Lounge.

She began offering up hints, veiled and puzzling, phrased in a manner she thought of as fetchingly ironic but which he only found annoying. In fact, there was very little about this woman of which he could approve; he had even come to sympathize a little with the Polish software salesman who had, until recently, made her life such a torment. Still, when she uttered the words "I like men with black hair," that line of liquid within him rose to a bubble. She had glanced at his hair after she'd said it; did that mean she was speaking of him particularly, or merely noticing, and with even a touch of surprise, that he happened to possess black hair himself?

One day in February the HMO newsletter, a monthly publication, featured a photograph of the office staff. By four or five inches the tallest, Theo hovered above the others, looking pale, and tilting slightly to the side. "So this is how I appear," he thought when he saw it, and touched his own face. This man in the photograph made him ashamed. His hair had become like a woman's, overly coiffed, as though in danger of taking wing. His eyes seemed foolish, off center, too eager to please. Yet each of these elements that disturbed him he could trace to a specific choice: he had, indeed, chosen to have his hair cut that way, had requested the stylist, in an excess of vanity, to do this and that. No one had come and descended on him and taken over his body; something else had done it. "You looked ridiculous in that photograph," the woman had said at their drink that afternoon. And then she had laughed, at this other, official version of him, and it had reassured him somehow.

Finally, things came to a head. They were standing one afternoon in the parking lot beside her car. There was the feel of false spring to the day, the sudden elusive lightness of March. He didn't want to go home just yet. The clouds were striped with pink and everywhere dirty snow was melting. The parking lot of the 999 was unpaved gravel; smoke was being emitted from a thin pipe in the roof.

Theo stared into her car at a row of tapes in a box. What did she listen to on the way home? He peered closer into the window, trying to see. She was standing on the opposite side of the car, in a black coat with the collar turned up.

Her little head peeked out of the thick collar like a cap too small for her. The day was affecting him in funny ways; he felt the desire to dance, to run, to puff out his chest and spread his arms. But everything he could imagine doing would look silly, here in the parking lot. Suddenly she seemed his friend. He told her his desires and she laughed. "Go on and dance, no one's looking."

And when he didn't, but looked at her as if to explain why this was impossible: "Well, come into the car, we'll pop in a tape, you can *pretend* you're dancing."

He stepped in. The car was new, and smelled heavily of upholstery. She placed a tape in the chamber, turned up the volume, and soon there was a woman's voice, husky and plaintive and at the same time advertising its own self-reliance. She sang about being in a bar and not wanting a certain man to come around. There was something that must have seemed comical in the intensity with which Theo listened, because the woman laughed at him. At the same time, she sang along, and he watched her eyes fasten on these lyrics as she sang them. Apparently, this was a real world, a world in which women sat and waited and hoped, and did not recognize, or seem troubled by, the transience of their own existences. He felt like his father in this reaction, a man who had known only a thick world, loyalty and family and self-denial. "Please don't come through that door," the woman sang, and he hung on her every word. He had re-created his father's world, then been unable to live in it. Some boy was pounding his way out, insisting on his prerogative to sit in cars with careless, hard-drinking women, claiming his right to the thin world.

"So, is it ever going to happen between us?" the woman asked when the song was over. She giggled a little bit afterward, as if she were only half serious, or wanted to appear so.

He reached out to touch the knob on the cassette player, as if to lower the music, to hear her better. There was a thudding in his heart that made him worry. He took her tiny hands in his own. The veins were blue and stood out. How did the blood get anywhere? It was as if, in this moment, she were frail enough that she needed him just to allow her to live. Then another song came on and he half-listened, and remembered that this was a woman who'd had three marriages and knew how to take care of herself. A former husband had once poured a bottle of beer over her head and she had slugged him. The same man had, at another time, suggested that a kielbasa keep them company in bed. He was in an absurd situation. Then her lips came to his and something else was momentarily true. She was really quite wonderful. He felt for her, and her body made the lithe, adaptive movement of an infant being lifted. The smallness of her face stunned and excited him. He said something, with his lips closed against her forehead, and did not know what he said. Still, he felt incriminated by it, as if it were the words that had escaped, and not the kisses and the embrace, that marked this moment in time and space. He thought if he could catch the words as they bounced around the car and call them back, then nothing would have happened. There followed a moment of extreme confusion. He looked out the window and saw a school bus pass. It was empty, but after it had gone he swore to himself he'd seen his daughter's face pasted against the window, staring out.

II

In the months afterward, when the difficulty of his situation began to creep up on him, he once or twice tried to lighten it by calculating that if Anna were an absentminded shopper, and asked him, three days a week, to stop at the supermarket after work and pick up a few items, the time spent in such a task, given traffic and the lines of shoppers he would have to endure, would be roughly comparable to his time spent in the woman's bed. So instead of buying tomatoes and toilet paper, he was satisfying a woman. But it was rare that he was able to think this lightly of it. Mostly, he saw the affair in darker terms, and though it was true (perhaps) that he'd been seduced, he understood that something kept him in it that was neither innocent nor powerless, but that had its own reasons for wishing things to remain as they were.

He had a secret life; that was the nub of it. But then he'd always had one, even before the woman had giggled and offered herself to him. The fact was that something in him had always resisted the separate enclosures of his life as husband, as father, as administrator: in his view, they added up to less than a whole. The missing chink was secretive and had to be sought out. It was what got him out of bed after lovemaking with Anna, got him down into a chair and into conversation with Acheson, with George Marshall. Some voice inside him emitted disapproval of what he was, what he had become, so that even in the intimacies of his marriage, the one place where he might have expected to be free from it, he was frequently bad-tempered, and harbored private suspicions as to his adequacy as a lover. He kept a part of himself back, and even in the most ardent conjugal embraces it became a difficult thing for him to say, "This is entirely me." Instead, he had the sensation of taking leave of some responsibility, as if for a child or a dog, while retaining the vaguest suspicion that, once the embrace was past, he would have to go and locate his lost charge.

In the midst of silly, mean-spirited domestic battles, it was all the more vivid: a higher agency of his would claim, "This sort of thing won't happen once I become a historian again." And still, there was no chance, and he knew there was no chance of that happening, and made not even the slightest inquiries as to the possibilities of its happening. It had become a metaphor for all he couldn't accede to, that was all, a metaphor he saw and recognized but still could do nothing about. And he felt something pitiful in the fact that when an opportunity arose to act on his secret yearnings, it was only another woman, that most conventional of lapses.

He was fortunate at least in believing his situation uncomplicated by love. Love he retained for Anna, who existed for him, whatever his hesitations, in a separate room, to which he brought offerings of what he considered immense respect, which was the same thing as thinking of her in sanctified terms. She was too good for him, while the other woman was not good enough, and it amused him to think he was probably most himself not in the company of either of them, but in the car, shuttling between them.

As the months went by, he continued to be baffled by this other woman. She seemed to care most deeply about her own car, which was always immaculate, and was frequently running it into the shop so that certain barely detectable knocks and faulty rhythms could be adjusted. The accumulations of her thirty-nine years came to less than could fill a room: a bed, a couple of stuffed chairs, some books, and a bureau. Once, she showed him a scrapbook containing photographs of her youth: a skinny child, blond, moon-faced mother, father here and there, without continuity. There were pools, backyards without trees. She'd grown up in west Texas, and the landscape was like *Giant:* her parents, spiky plants whose roots did not extend below the topsoil, seemed always about to disappear into the vast unmanageable light. All right, so not everyone was Jewish, but he retained the sentimental belief that everyone at least had parents who were big and crowding; from the photographs, it seemed this girl had always been given nothing but room. Three husbands, all of them crazy in some way, had cut out on her. She laughed and said, "I live for love," mocking herself. But he believed her. This life seemed to suit her; she swam in it and did not complain.

And if there was no love, there was something else: the sense that she held, in her knobby little head, a key to his undiluted potential. Perhaps he was fooling himself in this—what potential?—but there were times, in bed with her, that he caught glimpses of a second existence, played out along clearer, less muddled lines than the first. It was not the buried historian he was discovering, but something more basic. He *liked* this. Liked, as well, the fetching way she had of moving about her own kitchen, her hair cut short, genuinely and boundlessly affectionate toward him. That these scenes should be occurring while a baby grew in Anna's belly, he refused most of the time to admit. A first pregnancy you pay strict attention to, but it was his sad observation that a second, or—God forbid—a third, lacked the power to deeply compel. So he made his peace with it, allowed it to rumble at a distance, a storm that may or may not threaten.

Then, one Sunday near the end of May, Jacob pushed his way down and out of Anna's body, a week sooner than they'd been told to expect him. He appeared before dawn, in a room barely lit, with red skin mottled like a leper's. The birth came as a reminder of something. He hadn't remembered Leah's birth being this violent, but Anna disagreed. You forgot. There was all this fallowness, the planting and the agonizing spadework of birth classes and cribs taken out of storage—you wanted to nap during much of this—then suddenly a tear in the soil and some obscene growth poked its way out. These calmly rhythmed and sleep-inducing domestic acts—for wasn't the siring of a child in marriage essentially that?—really did have their roots in a savage world. Standing there, holding Jacob, beside a sweating Anna and several red-faced nurses, Theo felt a sufficiency unlike anything he'd previously known. And of course now, he thought, even while trying to push the thought away as unworthy of him, he would not need to see the woman anymore. Not now. Those futile, pasty afternoons in her bed seemed, from this vantage point, watery, diluted, a stream too weak to hold life. Later, when they gave Jacob back to him, clean and wrapped, a small mummy who could barely raise his eyelids, Theo retained trust. A new child was all he needed, would reveal all there was to know, to keep him in place, keep him focused. He went home and took Leah out to eat, apologized for not fathering another girl. "You'll get along just fine," he said, not believing it. The act of begetting a male child now seemed to him ungenerous, if forgivable. Clearly, he'd done it for himself.

He took a paternity leave and didn't see the woman for two weeks. Or call her. It was an act of cruelty, but he could not imagine leaving the house on such an errand. He cooked and did the chores and tended to Anna. The dogwood tree, a biennial, sent out its blooms in the backyard. He took it as a sign of encouragement. There was the occasional doubt—can this feeling possibly last?—but he brushed it aside. His parents visited. One night when they were staying over, the woman called. It was very late, and he was not sure his parents couldn't hear from the foldout couch where they slept like a pair of old Indians, hollowed out. He resented the disturbance to his clarity of vision, himself as son, father, as blossoming tree. "I'll call in a couple of days," he promised, to get her off the phone.

When he drove to her apartment, it was to tell her it must end. On the ride over, in the car, he rehearsed scenes and made big speeches. He felt his skin was covered by a protective layer made up of new fatherhood and good intentions. That morning he had watched Jacob nuzzle Anna's breast, and consume so much milk, with such ferocity, that the baby had been literally knocked out by it. Theo had never seen anything so erotic in his life—to be knocked unconscious by a breast! The erection that grew as he recalled the moment seemed to have nothing to do with the woman he was going toward; it pointed back to the sheer, dizzying eroticism of daily life.

At first, it seemed that things would go well. The woman was composed, even jovial, and offered him wine, which tasted warm and flat in the late spring afternoon. She had come home from work just for this. They exchanged office gossip. She was not much interested in his baby, more in what this one had said to that one in the confines of the HMO. He tried not to be offended by this, and looked out her window at the early leaves on the trees, wishing to be outside, to be walking in such a scene with Jacob. The woman kept drawing him back. After a while he understood her strategy: it was to render all the small, marvelous things that had happened to him in the past two weeks inconsequential, as they would be, after all, to anyone but himself. In desperation, he told her about Jacob suckling Anna (an indiscretion? yes, he thought so) and she raised her eyebrows, smiled in a way that seemed only half-interested, and said, "Well, that sort of thing will pass, won't it? Soon he'll be just another snot-nosed kid." She sipped her wine and emitted a short giggle, as if what she'd just said had been a witticism of the highest order. The implication was that only what was here—emptiness, dull furniture—would endure. Well, perhaps she was right. For an instant, the thought had its old power over him. He tried to remember how he had felt in the hospital. Perhaps there had been one too many trips since to Bradlees—for nipple pads, for diapers—they had dulled his homely ardor, his poise. But that was small of him, and besides, who else was going to do it? She moved her thighs on the couch, to entice him. He had told his father he was going to the hardware store. "Can I come?" the old man had asked, dog-faced, hopeful. Certainly Jacob would abandon him that way one day, but why think about it now? He felt very tired, the wine working in him. At first, lying down as she instructed him, he convinced himself it was only to catch up on some of the sleep he'd been missing lately.

The fault, he thought later, had been in coming here at all. He no longer even enjoyed her in the old hungry way, was assaulted now in the midst of the act (in the weeks that followed, as they continued) with visions of the achieved perfection of Anna. She had become saint-like to him in the process of second birth, the entirety of her given over. He closed his eyes and imagined it was she he was making love to, and this astonished him, that in the body of another woman he should be seeking his wife. But this was false, too, since the real Anna was not saint-like, retained needs and vanities, and only wore the halo when he was betraying her.

In his favor, the visits did slacken. Once a week was all he could manage at first. Then back to two, finally three, their old number. It was summer by then, and the invitations had begun to pour in. His life became crowded, packed full. He joined a club of men who seemed finished, planed smooth, whose foreheads shone. The old Jews, losing hair, filling offices. They were a bright, positive crowd. They talked of the sports they played—tennis! basketball!—and vacations planned. Going home from these parties, you felt your car was full. A daughter and son, the vague smell of old peanut butter and dried juice. The woman beside you in sunglasses, ravishing, dark-haired, a matron. You rode the crest of the world—were expected to—while the subterranean, the dark, the perceived truths that, if followed, led inevitably to the destruction of these good lives, all this you were expected to ignore. He sensed the others, anyway, knew this, while he—a pariah, even in the midst of his great new acceptance—waited stubbornly for a kick in the head.

III

One night, early in August, an event occurred that changed everything.

Theo found himself standing at a party with a handsome couple—the Diamonds—hearing all about an island in the middle of Lake Champlain, very lovely, known by only the privileged few, how the Diamonds were planning to go camping there the next week—they did this every summer—and Anna had told them she didn't think it would be a problem at all for the Augartens to join them the following weekend.

The idea frightened him initially. They were a big, healthy couple, these two, a pair of doctors. Liz Diamond wore round, oversized glasses and, taller than Theo— indeed, taller than most men—adopted a slouch when engaged in conversation. This gave Theo the unwelcome impression of being borne down upon. Of all the men at these parties, Bill Diamond intimidated him the most. He had an open-pored, outdoorsy quality that gave to the proposed camping trip an unwelcome air of hardiness, as though it would be full of all sorts of manly activities in which Theo would be expected to perform well. They were pressing close, though, at least Liz Diamond was, while her husband remained a step or two away.

"Jacob's so small now," Theo said, and, leaning back against the porch railing, thrust his hands into his pockets.

"Oh, Anna didn't think that would be a problem."

Liz glanced past his shoulder into the woods, where Anna had gone to fetch both couples' daughters. The Mackeys, their hosts for the evening, owned land bordering state-protected wetlands. It was an ideal arrangement, except for the mosquitoes. Theo slapped at one, and joined Liz in looking for his wife. Then Bill gathered with them at the railing, moving from his pose of nonchalance to one where he seemed to care one way or the other how things came out, and this inexplicably touched Theo, and made him think better of the proposed trip.

He excused himself and went to find Anna. He called her name at the edge of the woods. She was not very deeply in; he found her under a sickly ash tree. Apparently Jacob, in the Snugli, had gotten scratched by a low-lying branch. She was hushing him. She had worn white. The evening air was soft and the music from the party, at this distance, low, a jazz piece full of lazy-sounding, tremulous horns. When he first caught sight of Anna, what came to him was the notion of an apology, which, since as far as she knew he had done nothing wrong, would have been entirely inappropriate. Still, it was there, hovering like the dark notes he could hear at the edge of the music.

"What's this about camping?" he asked. It came out sounding harsher than he'd intended.

She looked up at him in the midst of thoughts as secret as his own. She'd brushed something away from her face, and he swore she'd been speaking aloud—he'd interrupted her—and not to Jacob, but to herself.

Then, too, there was this: tears were running down her cheeks, and the sound that came from her, as she turned away to hide from him, was a strangulated sob.

So Anna had a secret, too, though she afterward claimed not to. Her excuse was the conventional woman's excuse, the onset of an uncontrollable and finally unknowable emotion that overcame her at inappropriate moments. At parties. She had not needed at that instant to go into the woods to find Leah. She said she had felt it coming, the need to cry, just as the Diamonds had begun pressing her about the camping trip. So she had agreed, hastily, and made her escape.

They talked about it that night in bed and he was almost

satisfied by her excuses. They even made love, but he had the sense it was only because she wanted to mollify him, keep his curiosity at bay; for him, it was like making love with one eye open, suspiciously. Afterward, though, he lay beside her and did not feel the compulsion to get up, as he normally did, and go and sit in his chair.

It went on this way for several days, with him tender and questioning and her keeping him at a distance. It was nothing, she insisted, putting him off in that old, brusque, no-nonsense way of hers. But it was no good. His attentiveness was like that of a husband whose wife is ill. He might even have taken her temperature if that weren't ridiculously beside the point. He noted her paleness, her air of quiet. Had she somehow found out about him? No, she would have said, he was certain.

In the meantime, they were apparently going camping. Theo's concentration on Anna, and Anna's on her own pain, was such that by the time the Diamonds called, there was no convenient excuse to give. They had simply forgotten to talk about it.

When he mentioned this to the woman, she laughed out loud. "You? Camping?" It was hilarious to her. They were in bed, and naked, so his defenses were limited. She seemed to consider all such family outings objects suitable for scorn, and him within them a laughable character. What did she do with her weekends? he often asked. She'd raise her eyebrows rakishly and allude to a life she kept private.

They left to go camping on a Friday. The weather was fine, and Jacob complied with their wishes by falling asleep as soon as they were on the highway. This was rare, so Anna took advantage of it by closing her eyes. Very soon she, too, was asleep. Theo tried to interest Leah in playing some highway game, spotting red cars and such. She had a stack of books beside her and treated them like a fat roll of Oreos, to be devoured one after another. So he was on his own. Look at these hills! he thought, unaccountably depressed by the sight. For miles, nothing changed. A while ago, Theo, spotting a bird with what seemed an unusually broad wingspan, had pointed up and turned to Leah excitedly. "Look, a hawk!" She had looked, more to appease him than out of any interest of her own. And who was to say it was a hawk, anyway? And what, to take the question as far as it could go, was a "hawk" that everyone should be so excited in sighting one?

Just as they were beginning to close the distance to their destination, Jacob woke up and began screaming. Anna opened her eyes, but ignored the child for the remainder of the drive, didn't even turn around until they had arrived, fifteen minutes later, at the stopping-off place. By then they were all sweat-soaked and miserable, and so barely able to appreciate the body of water, marvelously blue and sparkling, before them. The little ferry waited for them in its slip—passengers only, no cars on *this* island!—a small crowd already onboard. Healthy people in good, expensive sporting clothes, and the Augartens among them, feeling out of sorts, as though they didn't belong on this boat, and how had they possibly gotten here? Their ears were still ringing from the ordeal in the car. The little ferry took off, rounded the tip of the cape, then opened onto a scene so astonishingly beautiful that Theo felt the rigors of the trip falling off him almost instantaneously. The island they were heading toward appeared smoky, ash green in the distance. "This is the forest primeval," Theo thought to himself, and chuckled. The hills bordering the lake, quite distant now, seemed Tyrolean, fairy-tale. With the heel of his thumb, he brushed the sweat off Anna's forehead, then kissed it. Kissed Jacob, too. What the hell, kissed all of them. He looked around the boat again, this time feeling one with the privileged others. Wasn't this a presentiment of sorts, a reminder that whatever might be true on the little domestic front, there was always this big lush world waiting to absorb them? And why not let it?

Theo amused himself, as they limped across the strait, by imagining the woman, his woman, onboard this boat. There was no place for her here, and that was what seemed marvelous about it. He could just see her, frail shoulders, little blond head, and skin too delicate to withstand this much exposure. She'd be sullen, critical of everything she saw, and in that way the physical world would achieve its triumph over her. Because—look!—if this—lake, mountains, air—wasn't better than what this woman had to offer, he didn't know what was. He was proud of his little family, whose skin could take the heat.

The Diamonds weren't there to meet them on the dock—they'd said they probably wouldn't be—but the woman at the information booth gave them directions on how to get to the site. They lugged their gear and found it easily. Liz Diamond was waiting with her youngest child, a girl, nearly two. The older children were off fetching water for the night, and Bill had gone for a run.

The first problem was to find a place for their tent. Exposed roots rose all over the place, and the widest, smoothest clearing was directly under a tree. Theo hammered in stakes, doubtful that he'd made the right choice.

The tent was up and they were unrolling sleeping bags when Bill Diamond returned from his run.

"Do you think that's wise?" the Doctor asked.

"What?"

"Right under the tree? Suppose there's a storm?"

"Then we'll stay dry." Theo laughed, excusing his blunder. The Doctor was unamused.

"That branch right above you looks dead."

Theo glanced up. Many of the branches had failed to flower, but the one poised directly over the tent looked most ominous. Would he have to pull up stakes?

"Well, at least the forecast is good," the Doctor said, letting him off the hook. "Care for a swim?"

They walked down to the water's edge. The Doctor was wearing green and black bicycling shorts, the kind that were supposed to breathe but that always looked suffocating. Also, it had to be admitted, the kind that made a virtual advertisement of the wearer's genitals. Theo's trunks were Hawaiian print, and loose.

It was clear, cold water that felt invigorating and safe. You wouldn't drown here, because there was a long shelf. As far out as they swam, and they might have swum 500 feet, he could still touch. He knew this because he kept putting his foot down, to be sure. There was no place like this. For miles, it seemed, the lake stretched out, pale and absolutely still in the late-afternoon light. Then hills rose. Where in the world were they? The Doctor stopped and treaded water. (He would have to stop thinking of the man as "the Doctor.") Theo smiled, paddling in place. This was what was expected, he guessed, to smile and shut up. Meanwhile, the thought arose, unsolicited: teach me how to live.

"We saw a hawk on the way here," Theo said, as though discussion of hawks would be just the thing now.

The Doctor—*Bill*—looked at him, one eye closed and— if Theo wasn't mistaken—suspicious.

"At least, I *think* it was a hawk."

The Doctor went under. Theo was left with what now seemed his ridiculous statement. He had never cared for hawks in his life, and to act now like an amateur Audubon was foolish. Perhaps it had been a mistake to come.

Bill surfaced fifty feet away. A marvelous swimmer. He submerged and came up like a dolphin, wide brown shoulders glistening. He had given up on Theo as a companion—that hawk remark had really cemented things all right! He swam conspicuously past Theo and headed for shore.

That night, they ate hamburgers cooked over the enormous fire Bill Diamond had started in seconds, using the dry wood his children, the two older ones, had gathered during the day. In the next site, a young couple Theo remembered from the ferry had set up housekeeping. They were blond and quiet and looked like they'd been together all their lives.

After supper and the ritual tasks, they got into their sleeping bags early. Nestled in, inside the tent, Theo's family seemed sad, as though they'd been waiting all day for an event to occur that hadn't, finally. Perhaps he was projecting. There was no way of knowing. They were all quiet and polite around the Diamonds, like children who had no power to say what should happen next. Theo knew he was very far from sleep, not even tired, really, despite the day's exertions. He reached his hand out for Anna. Was it beyond the bounds of possibility that they should make love there in the tent, with Jacob in his carriage and Leah asleep at their side? Yes, probably, but he felt the need to rub up against Anna anyway. She was already asleep, though. "What are you doing?" Leah asked, disturbed. "Nothing, go to sleep." Against the roof of the tent he thought he could see the shape of the dead branch, swaying. "Go ahead, goddamn you, fall," he thought. He continued holding Anna's hand while his memory ran back over their earliest times together, and it seemed to him—the thought was very strong and appeared to have grown out of nothing—that he had never been fair to her, and always, even as a young man, a little panicked, as if he'd known what small capacity he had for love was going to be used up quickly. It had resulted in an urge, from the very beginning, to make love to her often, to distract her from seeing this weakness of his. Now it seemed that he had hardly looked at her during all those lovemakings, so frightened had he been and unsure, and when he looked at her now, at her profile in sleep, it sunk in that she was getting old, and that it was too late for something.

When Leah fell asleep—he could tell by her breathing—he got out of the tent and was surprised to see the lantern shining in the Diamonds' tent. He went close, but not too close, until he could just hear Bill Diamond's voice. The children were still up; their shadows pressed against the blue fabric of the tent, while their father read to them. Bill's voice was steady and unanimated and the scene had all the soberness of ritual. It made Theo want to go and wake his family so he could read to them. But such a scene was impossible to imagine; he would never have gotten the idea on his own. What was truer was to see them as they were, his family: three little strangers he had abandoned, and for what? The tent of the couple in the neighboring site was lit from within as well. He imagined a scene as idyllic as the Diamonds', a whole island full of cave dwellers perfectly content to huddle together and read from sacred texts. That was sentimental, and he knew it. He went and found a place to pee.

When he was done, he looked up at the sky: what a night! Down at the water's edge, it was even more visible, more stars than he'd ever seen before. The sky was actually twinkling! He felt bad for his family, but he had to admit it, too: he had begun to feel a preference for being out here, exposed. He couldn't stay hunched up in that tent. So he was a bad family man. He took off his shorts and let himself into the water. It would be something to go out to the middle of this lake and float there and look at the stars. Desire for a woman was on him, that creepy unsettledness in the chest. Floating, he imagined the girl in the neighboring tent coming out on the lake, naked like him, and the two of them having a little tryst. This was cousin to a feeling he'd often had with his woman, one he didn't like to think about too much: how, waiting for her on her bed, on days when he left the office before her, he fantasized another woman coming through the door, *any* woman, and he realized it didn't matter. At heart, I'm a whore, he thought to himself, and laughed, and made a clumsy motion in the water, so that he had to work hard to stay afloat, and his belly surfaced and he thought: a man with a belly like that is not a whore. Sometimes you carried around a ridiculous sense of yourself, a mental picture in which you were handsome and dashing, and then you caught a glimpse of yourself that brought you back to earth. Seeing his belly was like that; no woman would come swimming out to find him. Yet one had! No, *two* had! And why? He gazed up at the stars again, and in the dazzling profusion of them, thought he caught some glimpse of anonymity, of all these men and women running around fucking one another and making up reasons for it that were grand and profound, when they might all be just like him: waiting, in beds, when almost anyone would do. Still, one person comes in, and because there must be some reason for that one person, we invent one, and arrange our lives around it. Just like right now, Bill Diamond was reading some book to his children, and fools like Theo might believe this was a fine and noble gesture, but really it was because Bill Diamond—just another whore at heart; he laughed, louder than before, when he thought it—had to justify Liz Diamond's having come through the door, having climbed into bed with him, having produced these children.

Well, perhaps these sorts of thoughts led nowhere. He floated awhile, cleared his throat as if to scoot away the unworthiness of these recent speculations. Somewhere a dog barked. It might have been in Canada, that was how still the night was. There was something a bit spooky about it now. He couldn't tell how far out he'd gotten, and was afraid to touch down. What if there *was* a drop in the shelf, and he was floating above a hundred-foot descent? He tried to be brave, and stay where he was, to avoid the dash to shore. But he was entirely conscious of himself, and no further thoughts would come. Just one. Once, on vacation on a lake in Maine, he had made love to Anna—who could recall the exact circumstances?—and he remembered afterward stepping out onto the porch of the house they'd rented, looking up at the stars, and thinking: if you want me, take me. It was the ideal, he supposed: to love a woman with the nakedness of appearing before God, without purpose or will of your own. If you want me, take me. Some of the men he spoke to had started going back to synagogue, but not him. Sex taught you more than the rabbis, if you listened to it. He couldn't remember whether it had been before Leah, even, that night in Maine. No, he remembered now, Anna was pregnant for the first time. Oh, what a good man he'd been then. He liked to think that sort of sex was what children came from, an orgasm you didn't try to control, to make good. A shot without self-regard. Oho, he was climbing the intellectual ladder tonight. But where was he? There was a silence, like a broken synapse in his mind. Nothing came after it. He floated. He had a vague sense of falling off. His life had come to this, to not knowing. He waited, because any minute the earlier motion of his thoughts would resume. His arms made strong movements, as though he wanted to demonstrate to anyone watching that he was fine. But who was watching? Far off, he heard a boat. This late? Its engine died. Night fishing. He had come to the end of it, to whatever he knew about himself, or about anything. The mind lost its power after forty, that was for sure. It occurred to him that there would be nothing so extraordinary about a man floating naked on a lake, looking at the stars and thinking profound thoughts, and at the same time a snapping turtle coming along and biting off his penis. Such things happened all the time, he was sure. He stepped down and discovered that he had indeed gone out over his head, and this time, the thought was frightening enough that he began a one-armed crawl to shore, his free hand cupping his groin protectively.

IV

The next day, a hot one, an outing to the sandy beach was proposed. There, everyone seemed to gather quickly into appropriate groupings. The Doctor and his son, on the lake, played a game with rafts, while the little girls held a net in the shallows, hunting for tadpoles. On the blanket,

Anna and Liz Diamond alternated between bouts of animated conversation and longish periods where they lay back, silent and unmoving, to take in the sun. Only Theo was left companionless, unless you counted Jacob, who had been fed and gone to sleep, belly down, against Theo's forearm.

The day had a soft, smoky haze to it that made him want to curl up somewhere. A breeze lifted some yellow, crumbly leaves—perhaps last year's—and as he watched them carried to the water he was affected by a kind of displacement. Vague, unfocused, it still pulled at him, and brought him back to last night, to the memory of him and Anna in Maine. Afterward, he'd had trouble sleeping, as though an element had presented itself to be figured out, and he couldn't, not quite. The water was perfectly still before him, white and glassy, and it seemed if he stared at it long enough, this elusive thing might come back to him, sharper, and with words attached, maybe.

At the edge of his vision, he saw Liz Diamond get up from the blanket and begin moving into the water. She tucked her hair into a blue bathing cap, carefully, slowly, then, lowering her fingers an inch or so, rippled the water in a circle. Finally, she plunged. As Theo watched her, he felt a great, sentimental compassion for this simple woman, this mother, this soft, slightly goofy being for whom he had only good wishes; he hoped, sincerely, that she was loved. Once she had risen to the head of Bill's raft, they talked briefly, then kissed. From somewhere far off, the smell of hamburgers cooking wafted over the trees, a pure summery essence. "Let's go to that picnic, Anna" appeared in his mind, as though the way had been paved for them and was now clear, they had only to take the steps; he experienced a moment of amnesia, assuming it was all because of this secret of Anna's, this new sadness that lay on her like a second skin, that they had somehow missed the boat of family happiness.

Anna chose that moment to turn and stare at him. It was a direct stare, and unsettling. She had on sunglasses, so much was uninterpretable, but Anna's body had always been expressive. The turn of her knees had sometimes been enough to gauge her affection by, and whether she was approachable. Now he sensed an invitation.

He deflected it. His gaze turned up to the sky, absorbed there for an instant. It seemed, even while he was doing it, a stupid choice on his part, one he would have to pay for. Still, when he turned back, and saw that she had already gone away from him, he was relieved. It had been only a matter of a moment. He could honestly say Anna hadn't given him much of a chance.

That night, predictably, it stormed. Hints had been given at dinner, when the wind picked up, and the trees, shore-side, bent at the neck. Theo saw the Doctor taking note of this, but prevented himself from saying anything. It was simply too embarrassing to admit that he took the lead from another man as to how, and when, to worry about his own family's safety. Instead, he pretended not to notice the genuflecting trees, the ball of aluminum foil picked up and carried to the site's edge by a sudden gust.

There were still a few stars visible when they bedded down. Perhaps it would be all right. In the middle of the night he was awakened by the sound of droppings on the tent's fly. Squirrels, was his first, hopeful thought. Acorn husks. Within moments, the rhythm was unmistakable. Well, after all, he thought, it's only rain, nothing in itself so dangerous. Then came the sound of rumbling, far off. He clenched his teeth. Thank you, he said, in anger, to someone not immediately present, for your eternal dependability. He heard, by the sound of breathing within the tent, that someone, at least, was asleep, though beside him, Anna's silence and immobility suggested a tension like his own.

"Are you awake?" he whispered.

There was nothing at first. Then the small word *yes* dropped from her, unwillingly released.

"Do you hear?" he asked.

She returned no answer.

"The rain?"

Still nothing.

"Anna?"

"What?"

"Are you afraid?"

"Go to sleep, Theo."

"I heard rumbling across the lake."

"It's only rain."

"So *you* say."

He rose to a sitting position, goaded into alertness as much by her downsizing of the threat as by the actual rumble, which *had* seemed to diminish somewhat. He wished for its return, if only so that he could say, "See? See?"

He listened to the plattering. No, there was no immediate danger, though it could still come. He lay back down.

"Why are you awake, then?" he asked cautiously.

She seemed to have made a resolve now to offer him nothing.

"Anna?"

"Can't I even have *this* time to myself?" she asked, and rolled away from him.

Time to herself, was that all she wanted? But if that were so—a thing so small, so easily granted—why was she crying now?

He drew himself alongside her and attempted an awkward embrace. Her crying grew loud, threatened to drown out the rain, and he became afraid she would wake Leah.

As always, too, though he was ashamed to admit this, her crying roused him.

"I wish you would tell me," he whispered, and kissed her. In his voice he attempted to place tenderness, empathy, but she detected only lust, and shrugged him off.

"Go to sleep," she said, matter-of-fact.

"How can I? With you like this?"

"Like what?"

"Oh, nothing. Crying so loud you're going to wake the kids, and I'm supposed to act like it's nothing."

Even that didn't prompt her to answer.

"I think we should move," he said.

After a moment: "Why?"

"The branch above us. It could fall."

She made no response at first.

"I thought you were talking about the house," she said, and snorted.

"Our house? Why would I bring that up here?"

It was curious, and hopeful: the mistake, her assuming he was talking about something he was not, opened up in him a pocket of calm. The little domestic arrangements by themselves might yet have the power to hold them together. The *house*. He didn't want to push this, or overestimate its strength, but his breathing had gotten a little easier.

"Why were you crying?" he asked. He made the effort to be calmer, quieter, more serious. Now he could afford to be like her doctor.

"It's none of your business."

"Of course it's my business."

"Don't you know?" she asked.

He waited a moment; then, chagrined, answered, "No."

It drove her away, he could tell.

"This afternoon, I felt you were ready to tell me."

She didn't answer.

"Were you?"

"Maybe."

"Then why not now?"

He could sense, from the quality of silence in the tent, that she spoke out of a place where, metaphorically at least, her teeth were gritted.

"Theo, you're a million miles away. You're so locked into your head you don't know the first thing about anything."

When she had finished, he lay back again, and listened to the surrounding noises, the rain lapping almost casually now against the tent.

"Tell me what I don't know."

She waited. At first he thought he would again receive no answer. Then she turned to him. The lightning assisted the terrible eloquence of this moment by flashing somewhere nearby, then again, so that the darkness in the tent was briefly lifted. Her face as she regarded him was drawn, as though she had aged terribly tonight. He had married a beautiful woman but tonight he found himself bound to—he didn't want to say it—to a crone. There. He was ashamed of thinking that; still, something true was in it, and something *not* to be ashamed of. He felt a tenderness mixed in with his horror. He wanted to touch the dry hardened places in her face, but feared the act would be misinterpreted.

And as if this wasn't enough, it was only half of what he'd seen in that brief, firelit instant. As she regarded him, he understood that she knew nothing of his affair. But it didn't matter. She knew something worse, a fact about him, a truth that had been with them all their married life but was only now being faced. It had no name, this fact, no incriminating detail attached to it, but it was at the core of everything.

Then something rose in him, a kind of rebuttal. They were in darkness now, he could hear the sounds Jacob made preparatory to waking. They were in the midst of a storm, too, a terrible drenching downpour that had heightened in the last few minutes and begun to sound like bending aluminum. Yet there was no possibility of movement until he could say the thing he had to say. He dug for it; it retreated.

"The night in Maine, Anna" was what he finally blurted, but in a low, barely coherent voice, as though he were not certain of it as a piece of evidence.

Not only did she not say anything. He could tell, from the character of her silence, that she had no understanding of what he meant. That night in Maine when he had offered himself up to God had been perhaps the most private moment of his largely private life, unobservable by anyone. In the light of this, he watched it go backward, lessen. It counted for nothing. And did that mean that his love, the manner in which he had loved, counted for nothing as well? No, it had been there on too many occasions to list, a tiny opening in the heart that had been, afterward, quickly closed up, as if he hadn't known what to do with it. And it was true, he hadn't.

Somewhere nearby he heard thunder crack again; the cross-webbing at the tent's apex was briefly visible. Jacob's low, goatish voice lifted once or twice, working itself up to a good cry. And now Leah, too, was awake.

"Daddy?"

"Yes, honey?"

"Was that thunder?"

"Yes."

He wished they would go back to sleep. Let him have a little more time to work out this thing of his. Leah began climbing over him to get to her mother, and then the scream Jacob had been levitating toward was achieved. As if to top this, from outside the tent came a kind of movement, a working against the tent's zipper that suggested to Theo the teeth of an animal. Alerted, he sat up. But when the zipper finally rose, it was Bill Diamond's face that peered in.

"We're moving into the lean-to," Bill said. "That storm's getting close."

The Doctor hesitated a moment. Their faces were only inches apart now. Theo could see the man's hair clinging wetly to his forehead. He had experienced this odd sort of moment before with men, the sudden, forced closeness that occasions an uncomfortable looking in on the other. Theo could feel now all the difference in himself, the *true* difference, as though Bill were staring into the eyes of a strange breed of animal he was only now recognizing, and feeling repulsed by. He wanted to shout, "But it's true! Yes! Everything she says about me! I'm distant, detached, I haven't a clue about life!"

"I suggest you join us," the Doctor said curtly, ignoring, or not hearing, Theo's silent confession, and disappeared back into his own family, joining them in their little exodus from tent to lean-to, clutching sleeping bags, flashlights, each other.

Now there was an urgency set loose in the tent. They grabbed what they could, and tried to force Jacob's stroller through the too-small opening, cursing one another as they did. Finally Anna had the presence of mind to lift the boy out of the stroller and they made a run through the rain, and arranged themselves, with a kind of awakened midnight joviality, among the Diamonds in the lean-to.

The younger children they tried to hush back to sleep, but the older ones knew there was a show to watch. So, eventually, Jacob nursing at Anna's breast, the Diamonds' little one laid out in a sleeping bag, they formed a small audience of seven on the lean-to's lip. Protected by its cover, they were relatively safe, even cozy, though Theo found himself unable to enjoy this as the others seemed to be doing.

Across the lake, at irregular intervals, the lightning opened up its own jagged path. "Oo," Liz Diamond said, each time it hit. "Did you know," their son informed them, in the vaguely obnoxious tones of the young scholar, "that what you see is the lightning's upward movement?"

Theo turned to Anna. She watched the lightning with unabashed interest. It amazed him that she could look away from their plight to concentrate on this. She gathered Leah close to her and again he tried to read hope in the simplest of her actions. Certainly nothing tragic or final had yet happened. In the morning, he would get her aside, he would demand to be told. And then he remembered—the internal motion was like an elevator plummeting—that he knew, he needed to be told nothing, it was now up to him to respond. In his mind he worked at this, and worked, and watched the lightning as if it were nothing but a wild distraction, a facade keeping them from the true thing. And at every break in the storm he expected it would go away, and leave behind it a pocket of peace where he and Anna might be alone. Then he would begin to unburden his heart, though what the actual words might be, or how the thing itself begun, all of this remained the deepest mystery.

V

They decided the next day, in the leaky aftermath of the storm, to take the two o'clock ferry back to the mainland. As he packed up his tent, Theo noted that the suspect branch had held, but carefully avoided any sign of smugness. It would have been short-lived anyway, because after the packing was done, the little girls disappeared. He panicked—they all did—and then the girls were discovered huddling together on yesterday's beach, unwilling to leave. The two o'clock became the three o'clock. Clouds came and went. The whole island had an after-the-holiday feel, though most everyone else was staying on. From the little ferry, Theo waved; at no one, it turned out, since the Diamonds hadn't come to see them off. "Good-bye, good-bye," he said, and saw the hills rising on either side, and wished, for no reason he could name, that Bill had come.

They drove through Vermont under a suggestive cloud cover. Everyone dreamed, though not communally. Anna lay with her head against the headrest, turned toward the window, perhaps sleeping. In glimpses, he saw the stretching of her neck muscles, a delicate mole poised against her throat. That she would die one day seemed the remotest of possibilities (though there had been days, in his woman's bed, when he had wished for Anna's death, if only to simplify things). Something in her reeked of life, in spite of her sadness, and he was glad, at least, of this. He watched the movement of her throat as she swallowed, the in-and-out of her diaphragm as she breathed, arranging herself in her half-sleep, unaware, it would seem, of her own bodily grace. How had it come to this, he wondered, from the days in the restaurant, the shots of Sambuca, her old, daunting self-confidence?

"Anna," he whispered. "Do we have enough money to stop somewhere?"

He'd been struck by a vision, all of them in a restaurant, some cozy Vermont inn. He wanted to prolong this idyll, painful as it had been, put off for as long as possible the moment when they'd all get home, and lose themselves again in the familial routine.

Anna murmured, then drowsily counted what was left in her wallet. There was enough. Theo pulled off the highway at what sounded like a promising town. "Greenpoint." But Greenpoint, it seemed, was only rows of houses, sleepy behind overhanging trees, houses needing paint jobs, with empty tire swings and ancient, cracked moldings, and some of them, though they were far from the sea, with widows' walks. When they reached the downtown, everything was shuttered; the town itself seemed to have been sandblasted free of commerce. Good choice, he congratulated himself, this "Greenpoint." At the end of Main Street was a single light, a Pepsi sign. They pulled up beside it and saw it was a pizza restaurant. Andre's Pizza. An empty cavernous place with fluorescent lights hanging from the ceiling.

"What do you think?" he asked.

Leah's face was pressed against the car window, studying this bleak hole to which her father had brought her.

"It looks all right," Anna said, unconvincingly.

They went inside. Andre, it must have been, was behind the counter, rolling dough. He did not look up to greet them. He had a thick mustache and breathed heavily, encased in a solitude that commanded a certain respect. They chose a table from among the many empties, but tepidly, as if too bold an action would rouse Andre, he would bark out an order that they take not that one, but another. Anna put out napkins, a gesture instinctual to her, which softened the effect and made the place feel more like home. They sat under a blown-up picture of the Colosseum. Theo approached the counter.

He cleared his throat, for attention, then felt stupid. Andre was aware of him. Still, the man did not regard them even when the pizza was ready, merely said, in the deepest, thickest of accents, "The pitz-a." Theo went to get it. They ate stolidly, without communication, and it was nearly unbearable, as if the rest of life might be like this. What had he wanted from this idyll, this break from habit? His hope had been that the world would take care of them, buoy them up—remember the ferry ride, just two days ago? Now it seemed, inevitably, up to him. A man spent his life running from emotion and then reached the place—always barren, always self-chosen—where he understood that emotion was the only thing that could save him.

Soon they were finished. He turned once to acknowledge Andre, to ask for the bill, but really to *be* acknowledged, seen from outside. Were they all right? Were they a family like other families? Andre named a figure; the man dispensed with receipts, apparently. Finally, they were outside, on the town's sidewalk, under a deepening pink sky.

"Beautiful," Theo said, but cursorily; he wanted to pack

up the children and get moving. The stop had been a failure. But Anna halted on the sidewalk, Jacob resting against her hip, and stared down the street at the buildings, which received the last light as if being returned for an instant to the time of their glory. The sandstone edifices rose, the engraved lettering on each of them briefly restored by the late-burning sun. Anna's gaze was deep and long. She was having a thought, he could tell, and he wanted to know it, it seemed to give her courage. "What?" he asked. She shook her head. "What, we're going to live the rest of our lives in silence?" he asked aloud. She locked Jacob into his car seat, told Leah to put on her seat belt. "Nothing, Theo," she said, and told him to drive.

He did. She found a station on the radio that played jazz. "Not this," Leah whined from the backseat. Anna settled in and listened and they drove under a sky that had gone from pink to pink-and-gray, with an astonishing gunmetal blue shadowing the clouds. Soon Jacob slept. What a good boy he'd been on this trip! The trees on either side of the road bent into one another, forming an arch, and as he drove he had the sense of a long tunnel they were passing through, a thing suggesting death but which still, somehow, protected them. What was wrong, after all? Briefly, their great battle disappeared from sight, and it was as though the stop had done its work, though not in the way he'd have wished for, or predicted.

"Are you going to tell me what happened back there?" he asked Anna. He was remembering her on the sidewalk, her face looking as it had in their earlier, simpler days, the day she'd decided to go ahead with her pastry business, for instance: serious, and a little saddened by her own seriousness. "Are you going to tell me anything?"

Anna lay back, with her eyes wide. He remembered now, what she had told him in the tent last night, the severity of her unspoken condemnation: how, at the deepest level, he had never really met her. The large and fulsome emotional life she had lived had not been his. She stared now, up at the trees, and it was as if he were seeing a woman in the process of making some broad adjustment, who had come at last to understand that she was alone, that life would have to be lived that way, under different rules. And for all that he would like to have battered down this truth, altered the reality of it, he understood that he could not, and that something in this awful adjustment of hers was good for him, would allow them to go on together. He hummed along with the jazz, then stopped. What if he had, from the beginning, been more willing to meet her, more *there*? He hunted for the reason why this had not been accomplished, and the sky darkened, and it was hopeless, he could not know. He saw the past, and all his chances to have made it different gone, and it was terrible, terrible to think that she was going to stop asking for what he'd never quite been able to give, but now might . . . well, perhaps. Perhaps. He couldn't say. The only thing he could be certain of was that there had been, at least, a change, even if a small one. And within it, he found a single, equally small cause for hope: his life had ceased, on this strange journey, to hover around a secret, had opened instead into a territory encompassing terror and the constant threat of loss. And to maintain this hazardous position, he saw now, would be the effort of his remaining days.

THE CHALLENGE
OF THE POET

Billy Hopkins is our poet. I know how that must
sound, like we think of him as a kind of mas-
cot, and that's not what I mean. We're a close
group, and most of us happen to be in the health
field, that's all. Will Morgen teaches high school,
and Joan Klapper gives piano lessons in her home.
As for the rest of us, it's very basic: we consult on
diet, or study X rays, or else listen, for an hour at a
time, to the monologues of the bereft. Billy's with
us half the year.

Usually, he arrives in January, after he's spent
the fall semester at some university or other. Billy
was a Yale Younger Poet a dozen years ago; that
seems to give him access to this life of his, where
apparently the well never runs dry. I'm a nutri-
tionist. I work part-time at a clinic a mile and a
half from our house. My husband, Steve, is a radi-

ologist associated with a hospital eleven miles down the turnpike. That's our sphere, though I don't want to make too little of it, and since you've probably already added up our combined salaries, it seems foolish to try to pull the wool over your eyes. There are the winter trips to the Caymans, there's skiing in Vermont, and since we're both from New York, there's that whole side of it, too. But Steve and I have three kids and we're settled. A lot of my life is spent in the driver's seat of our minivan, shuttling the kids from place to place. Billy gets invitations every fall to go and teach somewhere, usually in the Midwest—Indiana, or Illinois, Oklahoma. In the summer, he's a staple of the writers' conferences. You see his name in the advertisements of literary magazines, and you know who he belongs to then. But from January through June, he's ours.

The women in our group are tight—it may be our way of surviving these lives in which, let's face it, not a lot happens. In other societies, women meet by the river and beat their soiled clothes against rocks; we, on the other hand, have the telephone, and an agreement to keep no secrets from one another. When he's here, we talk about Billy. He's our mystery, the only one of the men we don't really know about. I mean, after you've heard all about Paul Kaufman's low sperm count and Will Morgen's bisexual angst, there isn't a whole lot left to wonder about these guys. Not that sex is the whole thing, but sex is—I won't kid you—a large part of it. Sex and emotion and the fights and the silly, complicated money battles; nobody's domestic scenes are left undescribed. Billy, on the other hand, has no wife to tell us about him. He was Paul Kaufman's roommate in college, and Paul says he was vague and moony and pretty much a loner back then. After that, there's no reliable scribe to fill

us in. Of course we've wondered from time to time if maybe
he's gay, then decided he's not. Something tells us he's not.
There are the poems, too, which we've read, though maybe
not as deeply as we could have. Oblique as they are, we've
all detected the occasional female presence in them. Mickey
Kaufman says he has a long-standing crush on me, and
that's why he keeps coming here, six months a year, every
year. I say it's the basketball and the fact that we let him
baby-sit. I also say, more seriously, that when Mickey
Kaufman says something like "He has a crush," we're
revealing too much of ourselves, and it embarrasses me a
little. I tell her then that we can't really understand Billy,
and it would probably be better for us if we didn't try. I
mean something in this, but I don't tell her what I mean. It
might be the only secret I hold back.

My name is Ellen Conlon, and I'm thirty-nine years old.
This year is the big one for me—I turn forty in June—and
Steve's threatening to take me to Paris to celebrate. I laugh
and tell him what a great idea (I'm still not certain if he's
serious) but inside I'm thinking, Why bother? We'll get off
the plane and there it'll be, the City of Lights, and there
we'll be, two middle-aged American health professionals
with crow's-feet around our eyes. I'm sure he'll have found
out from his colleagues at the hospital where the best
restaurants are, and after we've eaten he'll take me back to
the hotel and try to make love to me like a twenty-year-old.
Steve is very much one for marking the occasion, and it'll
be sweet, but all the time I'll be thinking, What are the children doing? and my whole desire will be for the time when
we can get back to making love in our habitual, sleepy,
undemanding way.

When I talk like this, my friends accuse me of having

given up on something. It's how I'm known in our group, Ellen of the Low Expectations. I have a gravelly voice and a way of scowling sometimes that helps this image along, I suppose. That, together with the fact that I keep my hair clipped short and refuse to do anything about the encroaching gray. When someone's in a mess, largely of her own making, it's my instinct to state the obvious: just do this, I'll say, and your problems will be over. There's nothing deliberate about this persona of mine, but Billy has a way of boring in on it, as if he recognizes its falseness.

A few weeks ago, we had the group over to our house on a Friday night, for dinner and then a movie. Will Morgen had rented *Love Is a Many-Splendored Thing*, and with the dishes still on the table, we all lay on our huge sectional and watched it. I knew there was still the cleaning up ahead, and I was already tired from preparing the dinner, but I lay there and got into it, especially since Will kept pointing things out that made us laugh. I think sometimes this might be how the gay side of him comes out, the way we absorb it, even help him along with it, by indulging his passion for trashy romantic movies. Anyway, I stuck with it to the end, I listened to William Holden's final message from beyond the grave, and then, while everyone else was sitting around talking, I started clearing the dinner dishes. Billy came into the kitchen, and he must have caught the exhausted look on my face—that, and my annoyance that no one else had come in to help—because he gave me one of those concerned glances of his. Sympathy would have been nice—sympathy and a hand—but you don't get those things from Billy unless you ask. He sat at the counter and put a toothpick in his mouth and said, "Ellen, you look like you want somebody to take you away from all this."

"Are you offering?" I asked, because that's our joke.

"Yes" is always his reply, and then he raises his blond eyebrows and neither of us entertains the proposition for even half a second.

"What I really could use," I said, "is somebody to help me with the dishes."

Billy can be a sport, once he's reminded of the rules other people live by. He picked up a dish towel and started drying what was left of the overload, all the stuff I couldn't fit into the dishwasher. I stood there a moment and watched him. His book jacket photo makes Billy look like a movie star, a pudgier Robert Redford, and he's got this very avid look in that photograph that makes you think he's only paused to write these poems in between a series of breakneck physical engagements. What that picture leaves out is the odd, fussy side to him that manifests itself in the tiniest things, the prissy way his mouth sets, for instance, as he dries a dish. Sometimes, I can't help it, I imagine how Billy would be after sex, wanting to slip away, to be in his own bed, things arranged neatly. It makes me sad for him, the impossibility of imagining him in a simple moment of intimacy. But then he broke my reverie by doing the thing he always does, the thing that cuts into my empathy and makes me frightened of him.

He was running a glass under water—apparently I hadn't gotten it clean enough for him—when he turned slightly toward me and, smiling in that way of his that lets me know what he's about to say has some special meaning, repeated William Holden's words from the end of the movie. "We did not miss, my darling," Billy said in an undertone, "we did not miss that many-splendored thing."

He began to dry the glass he'd been rinsing. There

wasn't a whole lot to this interchange. There rarely is. It's the way he operates. We both even laughed, I think. The line was sort of corny. But Billy had said it in such a way that an accusation cut through the irony, and our little scene in the kitchen was altered by it. Billy sees it as his task to remind me—he cannot let it go—that the big emotions of life, its dark and necessary underbelly, are the ones I am eluding in my daily existence. He knows, too, that I know this about myself. It's not the sort of thing, for instance, that he would ever say to Mickey Kaufman. But there are times I wish he would let it go, allow things to be simple. It may well be that I have missed that many-splendored thing, but is it really any of Billy's business?

I've gotten this far and I realize I haven't told you anything. Steve and I met in college. Those medical school years are a blur to me, mostly. Sex late at night and the apartment in Buffalo and my last years of undergraduate classes (I was two years behind Steve), where I didn't have a lot of friends because I'd transferred to be with him. What I remember best is an endless series of walks by myself, in the cold, where I think I warmed myself by constructing the details of a life that I was certain we were moving toward. It's pretty much the life we have now. I suppose you could say I am the woman whose dreams came true.

When you are married to a doctor, there is a moment in which he emerges. Those early years were like me walking on the ice and Steve swimming beneath it, so that as I walked, I followed his blurry, moving figure below me. And then, for a little while, we'd each pause and blow against the ice, try to make a hole where we could reach each other. And we would. Then he'd go back down again.

He surprised me by telling me, after his residency was done, that he wanted to take a year off and travel. His father had died and there was money. We did England, Holland, Scandinavia, skipped France and Italy. In those days, in those sorts of adventures, I don't think you ask yourself very often whether you're in love. You accept this other person—his body, mostly, and the feelings that go along with it—and you say, Here it is, my life. I remember sitting in the Tivoli Gardens with Steve, one evening, toward the end, when we knew we were going back, we'd even begun to talk about having a child; sitting there, in the quiet, with all those lights of Tivoli around us, and feeling pregnant already—not with a child but with everything that was about to happen to us. This feeling was of course for Steve—at least, it included him—but maybe not for Steve himself. He was going to make my life happen. He was twenty-nine years old then, ready to be a doctor. When I think of him that way now, I think: *God*, and I miss him terribly.

I got pregnant with Sara the next year. My reaction to having a baby was unexpected, but, I found out later, not all that untypical. Having Sara made me afraid, made me want to have a job, someplace else to go. I went back to school and got my M.S., then, almost dropping with fatigue, had Rebecca. Rebecca made it easier, now there were more of us, the house felt not so empty. Bobby was an afterthought, he arrived six years later, and Steve and I, whenever he happened to bump against my pregnant belly, would look at one another and laugh. By then, that was how it was between us. We were glad to have a boy, though. For me, touching Bobby's flesh is as close as I'll ever come to touching Steve again, the old Steve, Steve of the Tivoli Gardens.

That's not the whole thing, either. I haven't said a word about our house, which is a big colonial, painted yellow with black shutters. It sits on a rise. There's a stone wall bordering the side yard, originally built 200 years ago. All of us in the group have good houses, old oversized houses, houses with special features, and sometimes we talk about this, and laugh, as if these houses were really meant for other people, the large, steady families that came before us. We're the burghers in our little town, we fill the houses that once belonged to sheep farmers and ministers. It seems odd and a little insufficient that we're the civilization we have now, these steady, work-bowed men, these women who call each other up and complain, in careful tones of irony, that we're vaguely, vaguely unfulfilled, that something we were led to expect seems to have eluded us. What this thing was I'm not even sure anymore. Sometimes I can stand at my kitchen windows and look out at the yard and watch my children out there—at least, the two younger ones; Sara's eleven now and has gotten reclusive—watch Rebecca pushing Bobby on the tire swing, with our Irish setter, Dorothy, nearby—and I'll think, I'll honestly think: What else is there but this?

I would like to describe this sort of moment to Billy. Something prevents it; maybe the realization that in pushing it, I might very well be bleeding it dry of real, substantial meaning. I haven't told you very much about Billy, either. Not nearly enough. Even the little scenes, the things he says, or manages not to say, don't fully express his power.

When Billy's here, he lives in the house of one of his former professors. The man is retired now. He lives with his wife, their children are long gone. Billy settles in their youngest son's former room. He doesn't say much about this arrangement, except that these six months are when he gets most of his work done. He also told me that he gets pleasure out of inhabiting a room that is like a shrine to someone else's boyhood. "Cusphood" is actually what he called it. "Everything in that room is about being on the cusp," he said. "There's a Dartmouth banner on the wall. There's an old poster of Cheryl Ladd inside the closet door." Steve, making a joke, asked him why he didn't replace Cheryl Ladd with someone more au courant, Madonna, say, or Sharon Stone. Billy gazed at Steve, as if he was just going to let the question fade. Then he turned to me. It was only a moment's shift of focus, but he was checking on me, remarking—we were remarking together, in that way Billy has of making me complicit in his judgments—on Steve's thickness, his failure to understand.

How it is that I did understand is, I guess, a mystery. Billy and I have never sat down and talked about these things. But I can see, without much effort, the yellow edges of that Cheryl Ladd pinup. I can see the faded look of what was held attractive more than a decade ago, the long blond hair, the too-simple face, the girlish flesh, a little soft and doughy around the middle. I can imagine, too, how Billy stands there, facing this poster, in a world not his world, entering the body of an eighteen-year-old boy. That boy has since gone off, married, had a child of his own. None of this would interest Billy. What holds his attention instead is the way a moment, a boy's fantasy, can be endlessly relived. You do not really have to step beyond it, you can stay within it; this is a choice. Below him, in the house, the boy's parents move shuffling from room to room, fighting together the onset of everything grim that is to come. All of that, the fighting part, the blind wish for life, on whatever terms, Billy could not begin to appreciate, or respect.

Do the men understand any of this? There are times when I want to ask Steve, really ask him. On Wednesday nights they all go to the Y to play basketball. Afterward there's beer. None of the women is allowed. Billy steps out of the boy's room and joins the world of men, and for all these guys know, it's never any different for him. They excuse the fact that he's a poet the way you might excuse someone from having to leave the dinner table to medicate a buildup of phlegm. *These things happen, that's all*, is their attitude. Steve has attempted to read both of Billy's books, but I knew by their placement on the bedside table, open to a certain page, exactly where he gave up on each of them.

Last Wednesday, after the game, I lay waiting in bed for Steve. I'd been reading a book, a popular history of Vienna I'd picked up when I was pregnant with Bobby but never gotten around to until now. I was just dipping into it, not reading it all that seriously, but interested. I liked the title: *A Nervous Splendor*. I knew Steve and I would make love later, because basketball keeps Steve awake, and because it had been a while, and I wanted to.

Lust at this stage of the game is a funny thing. I don't think of it as desiring Steve, especially. When he came home and started undressing, I watched him. There are parts of his body I can't look at for very long anymore. They frighten me. I know this is silly. He's just a man. But he's a man aging. Things are happening to him. I closed my eyes. Inside my closed-eyed state I thought of the sex we were going to have and it was strange, because the pleasure had already started in me, yet I knew if I opened my eyes and looked at Steve and caught sight of the wrong part of him, some of the pleasure would start to evaporate. Is this love? I wondered, and it was like, seeing that question before me, I had to push Billy out of the bed. Or else, say:

It's this double thing, Billy, this trick we all perform, a dangling, light-reflecting prism of an existence you could never understand. But why did I need to apologize to Billy? As soon as Steve got into bed and I started kissing him, I knew it was the aging, fallen parts of him I wanted as much as anything. Probably if you start examining the way the mind works during sex, especially during sex in a long marriage, you're dead. Sometimes there are moments of our past I fix on. A beach, or sitting on a bench once, a hot day in the Florida Keys, waiting for Steve.

But then, as I lie there afterward, physically satisfied, another part of me begins to speak, always, and I knew that night we wouldn't have the conversation I'd been plannning, the one about Billy. Instead, I lay there in the quiet, listening to the rhythm of Steve's breathing change, waiting for him to drop off.

The fact is, I cannot sleep after we make love. Something keeps me up, more alert even than I was at midday, as if a sound coming from somewhere in the house below has made me anxious. I lie and I listen, while Steve sleeps the sleep of the just. I used to resent him for this, but no more. I've come to understand that this post-sex anxiety is, in fact, a solitude I've come to depend on, even to desire.

What I did within it that night was to get up and stare out the window. The snow had been on the ground for a month, so it looked solid as a moonscape, and I imagined seeing Billy down there in our yard, waiting for me. "Okay," I'd say, to his gesture of invitation, and it would be, saying that, like a kind of giving in. I imagined going out and putting on my skis and loaning Billy Steve's skis and the two of us skiing down the bike path near our house. "Did you make love?" Billy would ask. "Uh huh," I'd say, and wrap my hat closer around my cheeks, like I was keeping a secret. "Was it good?" Billy would ask, and I'd just smile. We'd get to the end of the bike path and Billy would say, "Want to go farther?" Ahead of us would be a big open field, vast and perfectly white. There would be no tracks on it. We'd stand there, just looking. I would understand, for a single, thrilling instant, that I didn't have to go back to Steve, Steve was an adventure, someone I'd slept with, a figure in a long, densely peopled life. Thinking this would make me want Steve again, to feel him inside me. But I would choose to go forward, into the unmarked field, and behind me, I would hear the cold *shush* of Billy's skis on the hard snow.

It was that Saturday night, after the Wednesday basketball game, that we had plans to go to dinner with the Kaufmans. Billy had agreed to baby-sit. We were stuck in a particularly dry stretch of winter, and we needed to get out, though I can't say, when Saturday night arrived, that I very much wanted to. I was lying in bed with Bobby, reading to him, when the Kaufmans arrived. Billy wasn't here yet. I heard, below, Paul Kaufman's voice, which is hearty and likes to imitate other voices, likes to make others around him laugh. Hearing it, I felt a little dread, don't ask me why. "Read," Bobby insisted, because I'd stopped. I looked at him and said, "I want to stay home with you tonight. I want to stay with you in this bed. Can I do that?" "Okay," Bobby said, taking his bottle from his mouth just long enough to speak. He's three, and it's late for him to still be on the bottle, but he's my last, so I allow it. "You can't stay, you've got to go out," Rebecca called from the hallway, where she'd been listening. Rebecca is my social director; she worries about me. I am always finding my name on lists of parent volunteers for projects at her school, though I haven't signed up for them. "It's good for you," she'll say. Listening to her gently chide me tonight, lying beside Bobby's pink warm body, I fell back for an instant, enclosed within the machine of family life, seeing it, for a moment, as a thing that operates independent of a single will, and being glad of that.

Finally Steve called for me. I tucked Bobby in and said good night, then lingered in the hallway. In the next room, Sara was at her desk, the halogen lamp on, her nail equipment laid out neatly. "Night," I said again. "Billy must be downstairs." "Okay," she said. She's really old enough to leave in charge of the others, but Billy doesn't let us pay him anything, so it's a convenience, that much more safety. Sara glanced up and took in the way I was dressed. She's critical of me at this point. "Where are you going?" she asked. "Dinner," I said. She seemed to be mentally calculating whether this was a situation in which the way I was dressed could conceivably embarrass her, then decided it was not. "Cool," she said. I knocked on the door of the bathroom into which Rebecca had disappeared, gave my last instructions, then went downstairs.

Billy was drinking a beer in the kitchen. He had on a denim shirt and jeans. He was making himself comfortable. The video he'd brought was on the counter.

Paul and Mickey Kaufman were standing in their coats, waiting for me, and, beyond them, Steve was getting his on. I saw us, two suburban couples getting ready for a dinner out. I saw us as Sara might see us, as I had once seen my parents—even after a dozen years of this, it still felt strange to be *in* it now, this life where you do little things to make yourself feel not so cold. I picked up Billy's video. *The Asphalt Jungle*. I must have made a face.

"Seen it?" he asked.

"No."

"Fantastic," he said. Then: "I looked for something for the kids, but nothing appealed."

This was just as well. Billy's idea of "something for the kids" rarely works. He's made them sit through *Koyaanisqatsi*, *Barry Lyndon*, *Life of Brian*. Now they ask him please not to bring anything, to let them watch TV instead.

We left. In our coats, making our way across the icy driveway, I kept thinking of Sara looking out the window at us, and also, of an alpaca coat my mother used to wear in the fifties, when she and my father went out on their rare dates. We were being careful on the ice.

As we drove to the restaurant, as we waited the hour it takes around here to get a table at any place decent, as we ordered our veal forestière and our red snapper, I was a step beyond the conversation. I don't remember what we talked about—whatever it was, our tone would have been light, chatty, and if we sounded the depths at all, we would have done so in a manner appropriate to the cream-colored walls and tasteful lighting of the restaurant; appropriate, too, to the solidity of our lives. If we sounded the depths at all, it would hardly have mattered, because the agreement we'd made, the agreement all the couples in the restaurant had made, would always hold us in its grip, keep us afloat. So we ate and laughed a little, and once Steve said, "Ellen, are you with us?" and I put on a little show of energy and verve to convince them that I was. But in fact I was thinking of Billy, back at the house watching *The Asphalt Jungle*, and the feeling I couldn't quite shake was that something in that activity was more desirable than this.

I was hoping, as we drove home, that I could watch at least the end of the movie, that it wouldn't be too late for that. In the car, I stared at couples on the sidewalk, men and women slipping on the ice and holding on to one another. It made me think of fin de siècle Vienna, as it was described in the book I was reading, and how couples had once walked on the sidewalks of Vienna, and the men had been thinking about their mistresses and how soon they could get to them, while the women kept their hands warm in extravagant muffs and knew, or didn't know, about their husbands. And there had been hussars, regiments of hussars in beautiful uniforms on the streets, and the women had looked at them. But now all of them, husbands, wives, hussars, they all were dead. A whole society had died. An entire society in which men, and less frequently, women, had pulled hard at the stranglehold of the beautiful, highly stylized world they'd made, and that chafing, that pulling away had formed the society as much as the balls and the going to work and the formal greetings of men and women on the street had. It seemed to me then one of the sadnesses of the society in which I was living that there wasn't *enough* pulling away, that people, myself included, made a great show of having all the answers, and all that the answers amounted to was a kind of formal domesticity. As if all the great surges and engulfments of the centuries came down to dinners like this, in cautious restaurants whose menus alluded, always, to other worlds.

I was lucky. When we got home, the movie was still playing, and Billy stopped it. But the Kaufmans wanted to stay. They took off their coats.

"The children were okay?" I asked.

"Hardly a peep," Billy said, but I could tell he was elsewhere, he'd had to be reminded there were children in the house with him, though he'd been the single filter between them and potential annihilation.

The Kaufmans said yes, they would like me to put on a pot of decaf, so we sat around the table and talked some more, and as I glanced at Billy's face, I could tell he was no more in the conversation than I was. I kept trying to catch his eye to let him know I was with him, but it didn't work. My fear, I guess, was that he would leave, and when I thought this, a physical sensation inside me, one I couldn't quite place—no, not desire, nothing that obvious—insisted that he stay.

Finally the Kaufmans left. I was never so grateful to see Steve yawn. I told him I'd wash up, but he insisted on helping. Billy had gone into the living room to lie down. "Mind if I watch the end of the movie?" he asked. There was no VCR in the professor's house. "Wait for me, okay?" I said, and I could tell Steve heard that, his face made a little reactive grimace, and when we were finished washing the coffee cups, he put his arms around me and said, "Sure you don't want to come up?"

"I thought you were sleepy," I said, trying to smile and make him think it was all really appealing, except . . . well, except what? I'd rather watch an old movie with Billy? Steve has no jealousy in him. He trusts me, or he values himself, or maybe there's no difference between the two. I had to be careful here, though, or he'd begin adding things up. My detachment in the restaurant, then the resistance to sex. He chose to let it go. In a little while I was sitting on the couch, next to a prone Billy, listening to Steve upstairs getting ready for bed.

Billy had his eyes closed.

"It's nearly the end," he said. Then he sat up and leaned forward to push the VCR's ON button. "Sterling Hayden's about to die, and then all that's left is for them to get Sam Jaffe. But that's a great scene, an amazing scene."

I watched, but I didn't see. That is, the beauty of a film like this, which Billy seemed to revel in—his eyes, as he stared at the screen, seemed recessed, as if the movie were not being shown in this room but in a private theater of Billy's imagining—well, this beauty was lost on me. I am not an aesthete, things have to be pointed out to me. I watched, and I wondered, what was it about this that had seemed so enticing back in the car?

Then it was over and Billy pressed the REWIND button. He sat back on the couch and waited for it to finish. Once, he glanced at me and seemed to look me over, searching for something. The only sound in the room was the whirring of the video going backward.

"What is it, Ellen?" he asked.

I had no answer for him, just the odd hope that something might follow this, that he wouldn't simply take the video and go.

As soon as it stopped, it looked like that was what he was going to do. Then he stood there, watching me, and I could see a part of his face move, and for a moment he seemed genuinely interested.

"Is there something you're trying to say to me, Ellen?"

His voice—perhaps he couldn't help it—had a trace of irony in it, as if whatever I had to say would be, on some Billy-level, fun to hear, amusing for him.

"No." I heard my own voice, a little faint, coming there out of the dark, where I sat. I took in Billy's form and I thought, Hell, maybe I am fooling myself, maybe it's his body I want after all. It seemed odd, anyway, that if I were to go upstairs now, and undress, there was a man who would want me without question, whereas here, if I were to do the same thing, I could only imagine Billy turning away, embarrassed for me. That sex couldn't happen was part of what made things between us so complicated.

"Well, then," he said.

"Don't go." He hadn't started to move yet. I felt him caught there, in my living room, looking slightly uncomfortable, wary of what might be asked of him, until finally he sat.

"Well," he said. "Here we are, Ellen."

"Am I keeping you against your will?"

He turned to me, finally, and maybe it was the dark of the room that allowed him to hold his gaze. At last—it was what I wanted—he was taking me seriously.

"There's that guy upstairs," he said.

"What? Do you think I want you to kiss me, or something?" It was bold, but it had asked to be said.

"No, I don't think that, Ellen."

He kept staring right at me, and even in the dark I could see from the cast of his features how far he was from wanting to kiss Ellen Conlon, or any of us.

"Why do you come here, Billy?"

It was that that made him turn away.

"Oh." He scratched the couch, and made it all turn light. "A little family life is good for the soul, I guess."

"And the rest of the year, what do you have then?"

His hands fell into a folded position. Billy looked like an altar boy there on the edge of the couch. His face all these years had retained the thick, mask-like texture of those pubescent boys you see holding the incense and candles, thinking God knows what while they swing the thurible. Some of them turn into killers, and you're never surprised.

"I get faculty parties. I get apartments that smell like somebody else's socks."

"And is there a girl?" I corrected myself. "A woman?"

"Sometimes."

"Who is she?"

"She's somebody like me, mostly."

The way he said it—the way he seemed to abandon the words as soon as they were out of his mouth—let me know this couldn't be pursued.

"Do you ever hate it?" I asked.

"Yes." He looked at the TV. "Sure." But he was not maudlin, was, instead, factual.

"But you could have something else, couldn't you?"

"No. No, I couldn't, Ellen." He was still being matter-of-fact, enduring this conversation as if for the sake of something else; his tone remained light. But then his eyes lowered and his index finger stretched out purposefully against the knee of his pants. "And neither can you."

He'd said it quietly, almost as if to downplay it, an uncharacteristic moment of generosity for him. Except that he'd said it, the damning thing. Funny, I was almost glad, to have the air cleared that way, though I could feel the pang of a kind of truth making an incision on my heart, a wound I would have to deal with, sooner or later.

The actual pain followed, more quickly even than I'd have thought, and I wondered what would happen if, instead of leaving it at that—telling me the deep, wounding thing and then moving on—Billy were to follow it up. To say: Change your life, why don't you? I wondered if I wouldn't then want to go upstairs and curl up next to Steve, and hide. I thought: Yes, probably that is what you would want to do. And it wouldn't be wrong, not really. What was wrong was asking for the criticism, demanding that Billy wound me on such a regular basis, as if I needed that in order to respect myself.

Billy got up. It was odd, it was like he had just fucked me and now was sensing his proper exit: was I okay now? Had he stayed long enough? The memory of something like this surfaced from a long time ago, and how, afterward, I hadn't liked the boy. But I couldn't hate Billy. I even moved slightly to let him know it was okay. My head lowered and I lifted it and tried to smile, though he knew I was only making an effort, but that was okay, too. He left, quietly, stopping once in the kitchen to fetch something, or maybe to look back at me, I couldn't tell. Then I heard his car start up outside, and the late-night crunch of tires on snow, and then nothing. The world is very quiet, at least, this time of year, and I sat there, simply listening for a while. In a minute, I told myself, I would go upstairs. Perhaps Steve would still be awake, though I didn't wish for it. His warmth would be enough, the way his body moves to accompany me when I get in beside him, a part of him ever-hopeful. I said to myself: Learn to respect that, too. Hope and endurance. Those things.

But I knew, even then, it was no good. I am a woman, I thought, who loves the fact that certain questions can be phrased, deep, hard, penetrating questions that cut to the core of existence. I want to believe, sometimes, that I can follow them all the way, even into oblivion, if need be. But I am also a woman who eats in good restaurants, and sleeps with a dull, good man. A woman who cares, I hope enough, about her children. I am like those women on the streets of Vienna, chafing against the bit and caring, too, about fashion, about propriety; only half-knowing that the world they inhabit is going to be blown to bits, and all that will survive are a few questions.

I went upstairs after a while, and lay beside Steve. He was warm, as I expected, and I leaned in close against him. In a few months, I told myself, Billy would be gone, and all that will be left is this. Steve and the rituals and the breathing of the children. I saw the habitual life waiting to seize me again, just as Steve's hand, awakened somehow, reached over and made a short, expert traverse of my skin. I took it, and lifted it higher, to cup my breast.

Steve awoke then. He needed no more than the physical suggestion to go from sleep to a highly charged state of awareness. It is one of the things I like most about him, that readiness.

In a certain way, too, I thought of it as an answer to Billy: our mindless late-night lovemaking, the heaviness of our bodies, the grunts that mean nothing and, I guess, sometimes everything.

THE SECOND ACT

Imagine, instead, that he hadn't died. Not, anyway, in the sordid manner the newspapers reported, the great writer lying prostrate on the floor of Sheilah Graham's apartment, still clutching *The Princeton Alumni Weekly*. A heart attack is not necessarily fatal, and he was only forty-four. Much better, truer, to conceive him as going on, recovering. There was a doctor in Hollywood he had come, vaguely, to trust. Suppose this doctor had, in no uncertain terms, cautioned him against the ravaged life he had been living, and as a result, Scott Fitzgerald made a change, a resolution, and before the California winter was even half done, boarded a train headed not for New York but for Baltimore.

Imagine him then making the long southwestern rail loop, bottles of club soda at his feet.

Already, good habits are playing havoc with his system. On
the train, he alternates between gloom and a billowing,
strange hope. He is going to the city where he completed
Tender Is the Night, where he knows, still, very few people,
where he will fulfill his promise. He has decided all this,
made himself sober on it. He purchases coffee, and somewhere between Albuquerque and the Texas border, experiences one of those false highs, brought on by a combination
of sleeplessness and the caffeine rush, in which his own
future seems, again, bright. He has been in Hollywood too
long, that is all, trying to earn money, trying to earn a
screen credit, being fed humiliation along with an increas-
ingly long series of memos from Joseph L. Mankiewicz. It is
some kind of miracle that he can still do this, still inhabit
the sense that great things might yet be accomplished. He
rides with the feeling for several miles, then places his
hands, unconsciously, against his breast. A moment later,
he smiles, understanding this, correctly, to be a cautioning
gesture. Above him, in a box resting on the luggage rack, is
the manuscript, half completed, of the novel he has been
working on, *The Last Tycoon*. He takes the box down, holds
it in his lap, doesn't open it. The texture of the box is
smooth and he runs his hands back and forth over it. "Cut
the rest away," he thinks to himself, and, inside, believes he
can hear the snap, the severance from all that has been difficult, and pretends that he is twenty years old again, on fire
with the ambition to be a novelist.

The doctor who had saved his life was a wiry man who
resembled the character actor Allyn Joslyn. Perhaps you
don't remember Joslyn. He marched, pale and moonfaced,
through a thousand supporting roles. He was the rejected

suitor, disconsolate in a tuxedo, outshone even by the likes of Brian Donlevy. This sort of thing, the doubleness of Hollywood, the resemblance of people to other people, always caught Scott by surprise, and when the doctor said the one thing he really ought to have heard, he was only half-listening.

"I've taken a look at your heart, and it's a curious thing" was what the doctor had said. "If I had to describe it, I'd say there are etchings on it, lines made, well, like with a penknife." Then, because the doctor had a trade of writers and considered himself, too, something of a literary man, he couldn't resist adding a flourish: "It's like someone's been writing with a sharp instrument on your heart."

On the table, shirtless, Scott had stared out the window and seen a woman, on the sidewalk, looking first this way, then that.

"So your advice"—he had swallowed, gotten over something lumpish in his throat—"is to cut out the drinking."

"And the smoking."

"Yes."

"And walk. For God's sake, *walk*."

It was what he did now, in the city of Baltimore, in a cold winter, a retired man, a writer. After his work was done, instead of reaching for the bottle and the handy daily abuse of Zelda and whoever happened to be visiting, he took a long gentleman's stroll to Mount Vernon Square, sat like a pensioned officer among the statues, and listened for some bothersome, incorrect phrase from his novel to surface. He limited himself to thoughts of craft; erected a wall against the vast, airy other side of life. Then, because of the cold, he got up and walked briskly, all the way to the Quaker School at the end of his own block, on Park

Avenue. There, he sat on a bench and waited for the children to be dismissed.

This became a daily ritual and the thing he looked forward to the most. At four o'clock, a bell rang, a matron came and opened the gates. The boys rushed out and the girls, walking slowly, wearing hats, had to endure frequent taunts and pushes from the boys. Occasionally, one of the girls, high-colored and with spectacular hair, stopped in her tracks to face down her tormentor. A daily game; he enjoyed watching it. At her post by the gate, the matron stood with pursed, alert lips. The girl was no-nonsense, however, and was never dragged into a fight. The boys spoke, yelled, begged entry into the hot, intimate circle of her attention, but she turned on her heels and soon enough they all disappeared, boys and girls, around corners, toward homes; the matron locked the gate. It was that bereft time of day, after writing, between rituals, when the temper of everything darkened and he thought of Zelda in Montgomery, released from hospital into her mother's care.

It was not a thing he wanted to be thinking of; it went contrary to his plans for himself—those good plans—so in the evenings he tried to distract his thoughts by going to the movies. It happened to be a decent season for American entertainment: *Kitty Foyle* and *The Philadelphia Story* and *Chad Hanna*. But most nights he caught only half a movie. For the other half of the time, he studied men's faces. Ginger Rogers came on the screen and the men took on a sleepy look, underneath which was the most intense scrutiny. It was marvelous to watch. His excuse for his own absorption in the lives of other men was the novel he was writing: he told himself he was only behaving like his hero, Monroe Stahr, a man making a conscious effort to drop away from ambition, to become like those men who simply go out in search of love. It was no good, though, as an excuse; the novel had taken on a life of its own. Something else, something closer to him was at work. He was afraid of it, and gave it other names.

There were nights when he followed young men in their after-movie wanderings. Most nights he was disappointed; the young man he had chosen to follow simply went home. But one night he got lucky, and followed a man in the direction of the harbor. The man was heavy, unattractive, thick in the legs, and wore a brown suit. Also a hat, pulled low. He walked with determination, at the same time hesitantly, as if he might reach his destination at any moment. There was fog, dampness in the air. Now the man had stopped; that is, his body had come to rest in a charged but absolutely still manner. Across the street, a woman stood under a streetlamp, looking like she was waiting for a bus. Of course she wasn't, but there was still the illusion, beautifully maintained, that at any second she would take out a purse and begin counting her change. Her hat, he could see from this distance, was felt, perhaps gray, and hugged her head like a loose fist. The man continued to study her, then moved across the street. It took Scott several seconds to catch up with the movement. By then they were impossibly close to one another, though not kissing or embracing; negotiating. The woman looked up, as if helpless under an assault. The backs of her knees wobbled. The man's hand had gone out and begun stroking her shoulder and arm. Soon they would go inside somewhere and continue, and the act, as he imagined it, took on a bitter seriousness that evoked in him an acute form of envy.

He went home and masturbated. He placed himself over

the toilet on the second floor, standing. No fantasy attached to this, but he did close his eyes and felt his lips form a word he did not immediately recognize. A moment or two after discharging, he was overcome by a fit of self-loathing, and remembered how Zelda had told him he was somehow, mysteriously, less than other men. He had long since ceased to attach to this thoughts of length and girth; she meant, he was certain, something else. He mastered himself, he flushed, he went and lay on the bed. Baltimore was in darkness. The shape of a water tower at the bottom of Monument Street imposed itself like a thumb against the sky. He felt for his heart and recalled then, with sudden clarity, and as if hearing them for the first time, the doctor's words. Someone had written on this organ of his. There were words, sentences. If he pressed hard enough, he imagined he could feel the raised bumps on his ventricles and read what was written there, which must be truth, and which would tell him the next thing to do.

But all he could feel was a stubborn beating, as if his heart had determined not to know anything, but merely to go on.

Soon after, he began writing to Zelda. Every day, as soon as he finished work on the novel, and before the walk, the same words. "Dear Zelda," and then something inconsequential. Here's how the writing's going. Here's what Baltimore looks like in the snow. He was after something, though its exact shape and form had not yet presented itself. The letters felt like wild, impulsive acts set against the order and duty of his new life, and he wondered about their power to disrupt everything all over again. Still, it disturbed him to read her stiff, careful replies, which implied she had not been unsettled by his letters at all. They arrived, her replies, on perfumed stationery. He lifted them to his nose and smelled her mother's house, the brocade furniture and photographs on the walls, all the entrapment from which he had sprung her once, a young man in a uniform in the Southern night. Or not exactly sprung her (he needed to release himself from his own mythology): it had rather seemed, in the Montgomery nights and for several years after, that life could be lived solely on the terms of promise. Now here was something else. A man with thinning hair sitting alone in a Baltimore town house, a woman recovering from madness on her mother's porch.

In her replies, Scott decided, Zelda was simply masking a fear of entering again into the old way of feeling, which had become for him, in the moment, necessary to explore. Yet what did he expect? "Your mother and I write to one another," he wrote his daughter Scottie at Vassar, "like people who have danced once at the Junior class cotillion and don't want to presume too much of the acquaintance."

Then one day he found himself smashing past the formality. "Did we love each other?" he wrote to Zelda. "I wonder now. I think of the summer of 1918, who I was then, what I wanted, the long approach to the house on Pleasant Avenue . . ." He put the pen down. It was an awful start. He recognized, at least, that an impediment had been pushed past. But that word *love.* He turned it around in his mind, uncertain whether it was the true thing he was after. It was late, he was tired, he finished the letter and mailed it. Then went for another of the routine walks. A gray pallor hung over Baltimore, the same gray pallor that had lingered now for a week. He went into the cathedral, looked at statues. Did we love each other? The oddness of the question haunted him, because on one level it didn't matter, they were separate now. Yet it was part of what had happened to him, this gift of continued life he'd been given, to want to make sense of the past. Love, sex, things he had failed to understand. The young officer and the debutante, the romance of it, giving way to a man in Baltimore Cathedral wondering whether he had been, of all things, *fair*. An hour passed, then he got up and went back to his study and began another letter. The question, he had decided, was important after all. At least, unavoidable. Toward the end of his life, a man seeks to undo the damage he has caused. It was an old story, archaic, and he was not terribly surprised, though a bit annoyed, to find himself inside it now. With this next letter, he began the overtures, the suggestions that the doctors at Johns Hopkins and Sheppard-Pratt might be able to attend to Zelda as well as the ones in Montgomery.

Zelda arrived late in the spring, nervous (it had not been easy, but an effort, to get her here, letters back and forth over two months), and when she stepped down from the train he saw an old woman. Hesitant, he touched his nose and waved. They looked at each other like that for several seconds in Penn Station. Strangely, there was not a sense of the past, of all that had preceded this meeting, but of the simple, clamoring noise of the present—steam, and the rough energy of an American railway station at midday, the surprisingly conventional clothes each of them wore. The moment seemed curiously thin, almost routine. Zelda's sister rushed up from behind, all bustle and suspicion, her hand at Zelda's elbow, leading her forward as if uncertain she would, at the last instant, turn her charge over to this man who had done, already, so much harm.

They had lunch at the Belvedere. Zelda, cold, kept her coat on. Rosalind, the sister, sat like a woman petting a dog in her lap. Rosalind adopted a slouch and eyed Scott as if waiting for him to spill his drink. It happened to be club soda with a sliver of lime, but he suspected that, if given a chance, she'd sniff it for evidence of gin. This was an old, old scene among the three of them, and it would be over soon. After three days of settling in, of talking to the doctors at Sheppard-Pratt and making sure that all the many things Scott had attended to for years would in fact be taken care of (and she approached this as if everything about Zelda's maintenance would be new to him, all the familiar things need to be explained), Rosalind would get back on the train and urge the wheels forward with her brittle worry.

Finally, the day arrived. He introduced Zelda to his customs. "I write between these hours," and so forth. "It's all right," she answered. Her smile struck him as the smile of a woman attempting to hide a broken heart. Had she expected something more? It was soon clear she had not. She took out her Bible and settled into a comfortable chair near a window. Every once in a while, he interrupted his writing and opened the door a crack. Zelda appeared placid, staring out at the yards and the rooftops of Bolton Hill. Returning to his desk, he felt the loss of tension: it was hard to go back to Monroe Stahr after watching Zelda. He found himself, instead, a room away, listening for her every move. For an hour, he traced doodles in the margin of the paper before him, he attempted to write a graceful sentence. Finally, he gave up and took Zelda on his walk to Mount Vernon Square, to the Quaker School. "Look," he said, pointing out his favorites among the students. "Look at that one." Distracted, she blinked, tried to focus, missed what he had pointed out. He took her by the elbow, led her home. The nap of her coat felt thin, the coat itself unstylish, and when he looked at Zelda's face it seemed that he himself was twenty-four years old, but that she had aged at a speed and in a dimension foreign to him.

That night, the first of their solitude, he sat in the hard-backed chair by her bed and watched her undress. In the later years of their marriage, it had not been their custom to undress in front of one another, but in the dark. So his staring made her overcautious, not sure which button her fingers ought next to go to, and she asked him to turn off the light. "Why?" he replied, and reached for a glass, which contained water. "Because I'm embarrassed," she lied. But he, in his chair, was merely waiting, patient, determined not to blink, in spite of what a wreck life may have made of her body in the time of his absence.

"Ignore me," he said.

She proceeded, was naked only briefly. He was startled, and nearly turned away, but forced himself to look. This was not Zelda, this was a woman he didn't know. He felt ashamed for her. It was inconceivable that he had coupled with her, her skin had housed his children. Her skin had gone spotty, there were folds, the breasts hung with a suggestion of illness, and it was all pale, abnormally so. She sat on the side of the bed. In her lap was the white nightgown, while below, he could just make out the tawny bush between her legs. For a moment he lifted his eyes and stared out at the night and at several lit windows and in the dusk and compacted glow of the scene tried to recover an ancient sense of life's romance.

In the silence of the room, he understood that she was talking.

"Will we sleep in the same bed?" she asked.

(Until now, she and Rosalind had shared the bed, he'd taken a sofa downstairs.)

"Of course." He nodded, to back it up. They had not had sex in years, sex was quite impossible.

"Won't that . . ." She didn't finish.

She put on her nightgown and lay back, covered herself with the sheet and blanket.

It was too much that he should make the same display of himself. Nor did she ask. Once, as young people, they had paraded naked before each other in expensive hotels, though always a little shy. It was one with the silliness of who they had been, the way they had gone about things. The couple on the cover of *Hearst's International*, gorgeous and mortally still. Briefly, the most envied couple in America. Sometimes, during fights, he had reminded her of that small fact.

Now he turned off the lights and undressed. He folded his clothes and coughed, twice.

"Your heart, how is it?" she asked, out of the dark.

Written on. Scourged. Impaled on a stake.

"I'm expected to live," he said lightly. He climbed in next to her, in pajamas. From her side, a heat rose. It was like a mild opening scene between Robert Montgomery and Carole Lombard. Soon, something would happen, he was sure, though what it was, what turn it would take, comic or tragic, this was the uncertain element. He was, in any case, far from sleep. She had taken pills to help her. The wild stirrings of the Baltimore spring approached the window, which rattled. Thinking her asleep, he got up to close it, then, approaching the bed, saw her eyes, wide open.

"Strange," she said, and he waited. "To be here."

⊠

Soon they had customs, an ordinary couple's religion of habits. They ate at the proper times, and cut their food carefully and stared out the windows of the modest restaurants they frequented. Once they would have torn apart their fellow diners, the pretentious hats, the ridiculous silent men, but now they took them in and said nothing, aware that they were as ridiculous as anyone else. An older couple, anxious as to the prices, sharing only the tiniest bits of information in place of conversation, declining dessert. It took an abnormally long time for Zelda to get out of her seat, to slip her spring coat on. Scott took a toothpick, and waited. He watched their habits descend to those of a class he had once scorned, and didn't seem to mind. The first exposure to the evening air was tonic.

Their lives could almost be said to be regular ones except, of course, for Zelda's madness. And madness was a thing that came and went. You could believe, for long passages of time, that it was not important. Then a streetcar would make a rude noise and Zelda, clinging to him, would have to be brought home, and any plans they'd made for the evening canceled.

Still, madness had been with them so long it had begun to give way to a form of nostalgia. Zelda asked, for instance, one Saturday, if they might go walking on the grounds of Sheppard-Pratt, where she had once tried to throw herself in front of a train. She insisted on following certain paths. He was struck, moved even, by what she was doing, by the intent, nearly distorted cast of her features as she sounded out some inner declivity, worked it the way a tongue does a missing tooth. Madness had altered, for her, the map of the world. It was this that touched him, the privacy of it, the way she felt compelled now to trace her own obscure topography on the old cow paths of the institution.

In the summer, he bought a car, cheap, barely functional, but enough to get them out into the country during weekends. Baltimore was hot, and they had not much money. *Collier's* had bought serialization rights to *The Last Tycoon*, though at an embarrassingly low figure. And there was Scottie at Vassar. Still, the WPA had seen fit to accommodate them: there were parks in Maryland where Zelda might rest her head against his stomach for an hour or two, and sleep. These were his happiest moments. He kept bankers' hours now, felt no compulsion to work on Saturdays and Sundays. Monroe Stahr was safely on a plane that would crash; Scott could see his hero's demise arriving on a set of graded steps, to be trod on lightly. Scottie arrived late in June, freed from school, to stay for a week. He abandoned the bed, allowed the women to sleep wrapped in one another, brought them coffee in the morning. At night, under the single lamp of the kitchen, they plucked strawberries from a carton, Scott in his shirtsleeves, Zelda laughing. To his agent, Harold Ober, he wrote, "I am remaking it all, just as if there were never pain and shame involved. Don't believe me? You would if you could look in our window, on the nights when I'm generous and walk down to the corner to bring back ice cream. We are a cozy little family, except, of course, for our ghosts."

During the evenings of Scottie's stay, as he lay on the downstairs sofa trying to hold on to consciousness an extra few minutes, simply to relish that much longer the state of his family at rest, the ghosts that visited him were mostly fictional ones, and it occurred to him that he had outlived them all. Dick Diver had been last seen driving from town to town, isolated and in decline, Jay Gatsby left lying face-down in a pool. In his imagination, there had been only a sudden descent from the cloud-capped tower. The world of the in-between had been peripheral, George Wilson's days of fixing cars while Myrtle screwed Tom Buchanan. He found now that he had to adjust his sense of identification. He was becoming like his own secondary characters, those for whom it was enough to simply hold on.

The nice thing, of course, would be to accept what had been presented to him and settle in, but he found in himself, on even the happiest of his nights, the seeds of resistance, and wondered when they might sprout. In a note to his publisher describing *The Last Tycoon*, he had written about Monroe Stahr, "He has had everything in life except the privilege of giving himself unselfishly to another human being," and it was this that he considered his own noble purpose in having brought Zelda back from the dead. It worked, to a degree, so long as he was writing. But there came a day, early in September, when he had to send the book in. A good day, at least at the beginning. In the post office, he hesitated, and looked into the clerk's eyes, trying to offer this heavy, good-looking young man an indication of the triumph he felt.

The clerk smiled, indulged him a moment, then looked to the next person in line. Scott lit a cigarette, hesitant to leave. A mural lay against the great wall of the post office. In a movie, the camera would have drawn back and taken all this in: the great writer lost in the crowd, the cigarette smoke, the mural. Then the package on its conveyor belt, going on to Scribner's. Until suddenly, drawn back into close-up, inhaling the pleasant smoke (against doctor's orders, but the book, after all, was finished), he was struck by the emptiness of his situation: the novel sent off, the day yawning before him, and all the energy he had learned to harness and put to use struggling inside him, with nowhere to go. He walked back to the town house, where Zelda was resting at mid-morning. "We'll take a drive," he said, distracted, annoyed now by the simple presence of her.

"Where?" she wanted to know.

"I haven't seen my father's grave."

This was not strictly true: he had seen it, but not visited it since his father's burial ten years ago. The old man was in the Catholic cemetery in Rockville, fifty miles distant. It was a destination, a place to go. There was no more to his suggestion than that, at least not at first, but she looked at him as if there were. He fidgeted in his chair, breathed out heavily, put his hand on his chest, reconsidered. But by then she had already gotten up to dress.

The day was hot. A street was being repaired, a small parade passed: it was difficult getting out of Baltimore, and if the truth were told, he'd rather have been making this journey by himself, savoring his triumph alone. He felt an impulse, a wild desire—not new certainly, but not for a while this vivid—to say cruel things to Zelda. They idled in the city heat. Zelda said nothing and may have been praying silently. It occurred to him that he could rip her dress without thinking. He could expose her there, in the car, for everyone to see, and stand in his seat and point at her sickly breasts and shout: "You think I love those? Anyone? My life has been a colossal mistake!" Such actions seemed merely a half step away.

Finally traffic moved. A breeze helped matters.

"Say something," he said to Zelda. "Say any damn thing."

She glanced at him and, sensing danger, closed her eyes, slept awhile. He drove. Arbutus. Relay. Horses raced in the depths of the Maryland countryside and the hotels resembled Selznick's set for Tara. The one-story, shabby roadhouses were more inviting. He'd completed his best novel, his hardest and toughest. It would be all right certainly, today only, to let go. But he had this woman beside him and he was remembering—forcing himself to, anyway—the last time he had let go with her, in Cuba, when she'd ended up locked in a room, praying, while he'd nearly had his eye taken out in a fight. Or had that been later, another time? He fought the seduction, swallowed hard, drove. But it seemed too cruel a punishment, to have finished and to be facing only sobriety, dullness, ruin. Would she like to read to him from her Bible? The Book of Ruth, perhaps? He felt, in his imagination, the sting of his hand against those cheeks, slapping her back into life. She was intent on hiding from him, and he wanted something, suddenly very badly, if not from her then from another source. He pulled over, at the next roadhouse.

The establishment was located at the top of a hill; behind it, the land fell off sharply. There was a wide circle for cars. He heard water somewhere not far off. Zelda awoke. She stared at the building, seemed to know what it was. Her anxiety took the form of scratching her knee.

Scott opened the door and got out.

He stood by the fender, lifted his shoe, looked at her. He was concerned with a couple of sentences in the book, wanted to call it back, would wait for Perkins's reply. Zelda would not look at him now. That being the case (had he stopped here only to test her?), he was going in to have a drink, one or two. More. There was no end to what he imagined. What was tomorrow, and the next day, what would he do? He touched the warm hood of the car. She turned to him.

Stop me, he thought suddenly. *Stop me.*

There was a moment then when she looked at him in the old way. A reservoir of feeling opened. But she couldn't hold it, or his gaze. It had given him fuel, though; in his mind's eye, he saw the battle he must have now, *must*, which would involve going in and getting drunk and maligning her to the bartender until he was thrown out, and then he would say the same hateful things to her, until someone drove them home or beat him up or did *something* to end it. And he must do this, he must hate her, though it had begun to seem to him, standing there, a source of infinite mystery that this old, pale woman in the car should require from him a punishment so severe.

"I should tell you that I'm going to write Rosalind to come and get me," she said, and it had a kind of debutante pout to it, something recovered from deep in the past. She looked as though she feared what he would say next.

He came around and opened the door of the car.

"Get out," he said.

She didn't like the way he looked, the red around his temples, the manner in which he was clutching himself, near the armpit.

"You shouldn't . . ."

"I don't care what I shouldn't be doing," he said.

He thought the line was melodramatic. He was dragging her into the woods. He imagined how they must look, how *she* must look, in the dress she had worn, gussying herself up as if for some occasion. He had no idea what his intention was except that there was nothing after it, nothing he could see, anyway. He wanted to be finished with her just as he had finished the book. The two had gone together, always, and he believed now, was certain (and wanted to punish himself for it) that it had been, after all, a false love, a goad to achievement, nothing more.

Then they were in the woods, and stood there, facing the trickling brook, which was not much, and which flowed at a considerable distance down the hill. Around them were wild strawberries, blue flowers, acorns, the pale growth of late summer. He was holding her hand, and in the gesture there was still the potential for violence, though it had lessened—he couldn't remember suddenly what he had brought her here for, or what he intended to do. She might not have known, though, that she was safe, because she fell against him, as a way, he thought, of escaping his grasp. She fell like a woman collapsing under the force of a man's passion. It was impossible then, from the way she lay on the ground, the way her legs fell, that their old sex shouldn't have reared its head. For a moment, neither of them looked away from it, but locked eyes. It hovered between them, and asked to be considered, and he thought, as it did so, that it was a thing—not the sex itself, but the charge out of which it had sprung—that neither of them would ever outgrow.

Finally Zelda closed her eyes and wished it away. In the moments afterward, he was left with it, with the summation of feeling, as real a companion as he could imagine.

Calm now, the air and everything it carried seemed held in abeyance, as if waiting for him to acknowledge what was left to be acknowledged. Crouching, he touched his scalp, felt the thinness of the skin, the thick veins pressing against it. How long before a repetition of the revolt of the heart? He rested two fingers on Zelda's forehead. He would let her sleep, then they would get up, brush each other's clothes off, and continue on the ride to Rockville. There, he would clear whatever dead growth was to be found around his father's grave, freshen the earth, and say something brusque, sad, and officious, in place of a prayer. The words on his heart, which had leaped up in the moments before, as Zelda lay below him, retreated then, having not quite allowed themselves to be read. They would, to be sure, have been too banal to speak. He remembered, instead, a day at Cap d'Antibes, the water of the Mediterranean, his hand on his knee, and Scottie close, and Zelda. Someone was taking their photograph, he remembered now. They had held their poses a long time, not out of happiness certainly. There are one or two moments to which one remains true. One neither moves forward from them nor retreats. He ran his hand up and over Zelda's forehead and said, with his hand, *Now rest.*

THE FILMS OF
RICHARD EGAN

The View from Pompey's Head (1955)

An actor, if he is to become a star, has to be seen
first in motion. Riding a horse. Driving a fast car.
His initial impression, the tipping of his hat, must
take place at a speed and in a dimension different
from our own. This is a rule. In *Lawrence of Arabia*,
we sit, for three or four minutes, waiting for the
blur at the edge of the desert to come forward and
distinguish itself. Then it becomes Omar Sharif,
on a camel, and something begins, a kind of love
affair. So Richard Egan, late of California and the
Philippines, makes his first bid for our serious
attention on a speeding train.

Forget plot. Plot is not important. What was
Omar Sharif crossing the desert for anyway? Five
minutes into *The View from Pompey's Head*, we are
made to see the gambit, the reason Richard Egan
has been spit into our faces. He steps off the train

and Dana Wynter is there, waiting. It is the fifties, and there are all these beautiful women to be fucked. Susan Hayward. Grace Kelly. They can have careers, but in the end it is their bodies that have to be soothed. Don't ask why, we can't go home until we've seen that done. And there are a limited number of believable practitioners of the art: Holden, Lancaster, Cooper, Cagney in a pinch, though he's getting old; Bogart, but he's dying. So Richard Egan, whose face may be familiar to us from supporting parts, steps up to the plate.

There is, at first, that exhilaration of possibility, of the new. Except that he is ugly. Still, he wears his own ugliness well, with confidence. He has a good profile. He moves, and waits to speak his lines, with extraordinary calm. Also, he is good at listening. We weigh these things, as we take him in, the way we might weigh similar gestures if we were speaking to a man at a party. We are holding something in reserve: a judgment, a willingness to continue the conversation.

When he finally gets to hold Dana Wynter, it is shocking how expert he looks, the way his hands go to the exact places a man's hands might go. He pulls her to him in such a manner, we wonder why the actress doesn't slap him, doesn't say, "This is acting, fool!" But she doesn't; instead, she responds, and the moment is achieved.

Leave it at that, and he becomes a star. But Richard Egan, in this movie, is a married man. Dana Wynter is not his wife, but an old flame; he has come back to the South to reclaim not only her but his own lost youth, and it will never do, it cannot be done, not now, not in this decade. We know he will have to get back on the train, in time. Still, it's easy to imagine the way Cooper would have handled the moment of renunciation: mouthing the penitential lines, allowing the deep familiar crevices to appear in his face, and still winking at us: I fucked her, man. I *got in.*

The great, enduring stars are careful, and take things on the journey that will protect them. But Richard Egan, at the beginning, looks as though he believes solely in his own luck. He is like a boy going off to college, or a bridegroom, as he steps on the train and waves good-bye to Dana Wynter. Nothing separates him from the story he has begun to tell.

You were five years old that year, sitting, in pajamas, in the backseat of a car at the drive-in. None of this was evident to you as you looked at the face, large and red on the white rectangle in the woods of Natick. In the front seat your parents, stolid, young, watched. About them you were certain, too, that luck would attach, and only good things happen.

Seven Cities of Gold (1955)

In 1955, no one lost sleep over the casting of Anglos in ethnic roles. Richard Egan's concession to the verismo of his part here—a soldier in the Spanish cavalry, in the 1760s—consists of a ponytail and the name he has been given. Still, when someone calls "José!" we expect him to turn around, confused, wondering where the hell José might be.

He looks good on a horse, though, and he has mastered the trick of appearing as though he belongs up there. We can breathe a little, those of us who are rooting for him. That confidence is really something.

He is even allowed, for the first time, a moment of fun.

The soldiers, on their way to the mythical seven cities, have pitched camp for the night, somewhere in the vicinity of San Diego Harbor. There are campfires, guitars. A song about Rosalita. Leaning against his own bedroll, propped on one elbow, he sings along for two bars. He wears a big wide smile that is wonderful to see. All hope for himself is in it. The young actor anticipating a lifetime of adventure.

Within five minutes, though, we begin to suspect that the sexy swaggering of Richard Egan and his pal Anthony Quinn isn't really what this movie has on its mind. A priest, Father Junípero Serra, has come along on the expedition; he has begun converting Indians. He smiles beatifically and dreams of missions in California. Almost as soon as Richard Egan takes Ula, the Indian girl, into the surf with him, we know, we know what must happen.

They have given him a scene, lines to speak, a credo to hold up before the priest after the Indian girl has thrown herself off a cliff, following his attempt to dump her. "I have neither guilt, nor shame, nor fear" is not a line he should ever have been asked to speak, so patently does he not believe it. When next we see him, he is reciting the act of contrition, and turning himself over to the heathens.

The Indians return his body to the mission, and a soldier reports, "They tore out his heart. It was a great one." But we already knew that. We may even suspect, at this point, his heart is too great, and therefore of no use to us. Closer to our own hearts would be a hero who cut out of the situation, claiming he only kissed her, he promised nothing, they stood in the surf, his hands went to the good places, she responded. He is no fool. He knows this. Knows, too, that, very soon, he has to begin to ally himself with the world as we want to perceive it. That is, if he wants to stake his claim. Even as he recites the act of contrition, we can see him planning a meeting at Fox, the words he will use, which he hopes will not reek too heavily of desperation.

Love Me Tender (1956)

"Let me get the girl," he suggests, not long after, in the office of an executive in charge of casting at Twentieth Century–Fox.

It is not that they have given up on him, he has been assured, but the first two pictures have failed commercially, as has a third, *Violent Saturday*, released briefly and unceremoniously the same year. The right project has to be found, that's all.

A silence follows his proposal. The executive crosses his legs, sucks a mint. Richard Egan experiences one of those gut-clenching moments when he perceives himself on the verge of being ignored, passed over, and that no second chance will follow this. So he repeats the suggestion, elaborates on it.

"I feel I can make contact with the public. With a large public. But they can't always see me as somebody who loses."

It is like a speech he might give in the movies. He says it that way, exuding confidence and calm. Briefly, he sees the executive as Father Junípero Serra, as a man who will send him to have his heart cut out. But the man sitting across from him is pocker-faced. He uncrosses his legs.

"Nobody's interested in typecasting you, Dick," the man says.

To prove it, Richard Egan is given a Civil War picture in development. In it, he will not be asked, for the third time, to deny himself. He will, instead, get the girl, and turn things around, become an established star.

That, at least, is how he proceeds, with that assurance. But a man who has failed enough times begins looking around for ways he might fail again. Not through his own fault, but through circumstance, mismanagement. No one on the set, at any rate, appears to be a threat, least of all the hillbilly singer cast as his younger brother, the one who loses this time out.

But midway through filming, something awful happens. The mint-sucking executive shows up, watches a day of shooting. In the evening, the director disappears. There are new scenes the next day. Not scenes, precisely. The hillbilly singer is given songs, numbers. He is asked to swivel his hips at the postwar pie bake-off and make girls in bonnets swoon. Watching this, Richard Egan can convince himself for only a day or two that this does not alter the plan, it is still his film, the one where he gets the girl.

In the rushes, watched in the evening, he begins to see it, to understand something about the movies he has not understood before. It is nearly ontological in its weight. He is doing his best acting, he can see that. His performance has depth and gravity. And it counts for nothing. The hillbilly is a terrible actor. He has everything to learn. But when he is on-screen, something quickens. It is that simple.

Richard Egan looks, through much of the ensuing film, like a man on whom something is slowly dawning, the inadequacy of his own heavy body, the unchosen trick of forcing plot and circumstance to give way to a separate compact with the audience. But there are still the lines to be said, gestures made. They must still be invested in, though the film he thought he was making has stopped being made, another film has replaced it, a far sillier film that will bleed into history and leave people asking: Who was it, remember, in the film with Elvis, you know, the *other guy*?

A Summer Place (1959)

A three-year interval. Other movies, unremarkable ones. Then the role of his career, the one he was born to play. There are chances and chances. For a moment, in 1959, he must have felt the world opening to him, as though, in spite of all the hard luck that had preceded this, he really couldn't fail.

He is so good in this. He found his audience, too, women in their early forties, women just around the corner of possibility, women as old then as Dorothy McGuire, the love interest, the woman he has come back to the Pine Island Inn in order to see; the woman who dumped him once, years before, when he was the poor lifeguard, in favor of the rich boy who has since taken over the inn. He is coming to her now as a self-made millionaire, while her husband, the rich boy, drinks and runs the inn into the ground. "I'm not putting on any dog," Richard Egan says to his uppity wife, on the yacht they have chartered, and we love him, right away, for the poor boy's way he has of saying "dog."

Then he has his moment, the one for which he will live forever. A heavy rain is falling over the Pine Island Inn, and the roof is leaking. An old woman, bothered by the dripping in her room, approaches Richard Egan, remembering him from years before. "Lifeguard," she says, "how about fixing my leak?"

Richard Egan cocks his head, takes a masterful pause, and asks, "Just where are you leaking?"

In theaters all over America, the line got a laugh. But it was not a joke, not entirely. You were nine years old that summer. Your mother dragged you and your brother to see the movie three times, and quoted the line to her friends, and wore a particular look when she quoted it. So you knew, just from watching, it was a question a woman of a certain age deeply wanted to be asked. And you knew, too, because of this, that your father had stopped being what he was, that your mother needed now to seek out others, in the dark.

Earlier, at the dinner table, Richard Egan listened to Dorothy McGuire tell of a dream she'd had. Women's faces aren't shot that way anymore, in that kind of soft focus. Dorothy McGuire looks beautiful as she tells of her old plan, the quest of the early days of her marriage, to walk naked on the beach in September, after all the summer guests had gone. "What happened?" he asks. "I simply woke up, I guess." She smiles, and then he just looks at her, a look stripped of everything but compassion, merely *comprehending*. For a moment, that look puts him up with the greats. And he is rewarded for it, too, allowed a consummation previously forbidden him. In the attic, wet from fixing the roof, he takes Dorothy McGuire into his arms and kisses her. This time, we know, he will not be asked to renounce, or to give his heart to the Indians in payment. This time, no singer waits offstage to nullify his efforts. We rejoice with him in the kiss, those of us who have stuck with him to this point. His wife won't sleep with him, he has stayed with her only for the sake of his daughter, Sandra Dee, just as Dorothy McGuire has endured a nightmare marriage for the sake of her son, Troy Donahue. Those blond, impossible figures hover over the kiss, those twin gods we will be forced to watch again and again in the next few years. But not yet, please. For now, at least, we are watching the restoration of the lifeguard and the rich, ungraspable girl. Dorothy McGuire must get her naked walk on the beach, and the man capable of restoring Eden given the right to do so. Just where are you leaking? *Here,* your mother said, with two sons beside her, and a part of her life past. And *here.*

Pollyanna (1960)

Consider it. An actor comes this far, stakes his claim to an audience, to the hearts of women of a certain age. The world ought to open now. Everyone knows this story, we've all read it enough times. A man suffers long enough, pays his dues, then he gets to not suffer anymore.

But in 1959, on a drizzly day in November, Richard Egan sits in a bar in New York, drinking with his agent, who has come east on business and who, at the moment, is trying to convince him to accept an offer from Disney. Disney wants him to play a supporting part in a new picture, the story of a little girl; the studio, it seems, is determined to make a star of Hayley Mills.

He thinks: *Hayley Mills.* He is drinking bourbon. New York in 1959, autumn, in the rain. Men in hats and the women who love him, under umbrellas, on their way to buses. *A Summer Place* has been a huge hit. All summer long the theaters were full. Sandra Dee and Troy Donahue have been signed to long-term contracts. The theme song reached number one. He is too reticent to mention any of this, to say, "My name came first." In the rain, the uptown bus, the wrong one, splashes the legs and raincoats of women waiting. They are far from the place where they can appreciate him, though he has the sense that if he went out now and stood there, a small crowd might gather. But it is too risky to chance.

He tells his agent he'd like to do another movie like *A Summer Place*, and his agent, looking past him, briefly melancholy, says, "There aren't going to be any other movies like *A Summer Place*, Dick." Everyone with bad news now calls him Dick. "They've just found out the kids are going to the movies more than the adults. So there are going to be movies like *Molly and Johnny Get Married*. And *Molly and Johnny Have a Baby*. Of course there are still going to be a few other kinds of movies made, because Lancaster and Douglas, they're getting old. And Liz Taylor and even Paul Newman. They're passing thirty, forty. So they'll find stories for them." He leaves the rest unsaid. There is that kind of moment with an agent, where you're told delicately, in the ellipses, where you stand. Such a person would not lie to you. Still, it is a great mystery why, with his last movie a hit, it has come to this. The bus arrives and picks up all the women. He sees across the street, in a lighted haberdashery, a bald man with glasses on the bridge of his nose staring out into the rain. And he has his epiphany: they have no power, these women, his fans, to make anything happen. He is trying to understand the world before it is too late for him, but he can only comprehend the fact that power has shifted, gone elsewhere. He is drunk enough to want to go out and hit someone. Someone young.

The 300 Spartans (1962)

As suddenly as it began, it is over. His trajectory. His gamble with himself: how high can I rise? And with the world: how about, consider, *this* kind of hero? It was vanity, yes, to throw himself out that way, but the war was over, there was that sense for a while. Possibility. It lasted seven years.

He has signed, already, to do a TV series. *Empire*. When a movie star does that, you know he's gotten afraid. By the time he arrives in Spain to don his battle gear for *The 300 Spartans*, he is capable of nosing out the potential success or failure of a project, and this one stinks of failure. Though the script is good. But the budget is low. All over Spain, there are movie sets grander than this one. The Moors' castle from *El Cid*. Pilate's temple from *King of Kings*. They are a small company. The director shot some of the best films of the forties. He was Rita Hayworth's favorite cameraman. But he is an old man now. So all right.

Ahead of him are long years as a throaty, nervous CIA operative, the captain of a tuna boat, secondary roles in which he will support the likes of George Chakiris, Christopher Jones, younger stars whose time in the sun will be even briefer than his own. *Empire* will fail to catch on, as will *Redigo*, his second series. After that, an even deeper descent, into the bus-and-truck companies of plays, sharing one- and two-night stands, and drinks afterward, with Eva Gabor, and Pat O'Brien. Then, the last stop, a daytime soap.

He knows all this, or some form of it, as he prepares to don the battle dress of King Leonidas. For the last time, his name will go above the title. There is at least that to consider, though by the time the movie opens, a multi-theater "dump" in September, his name will, in fact, be buried at the bottom of the ads, and boys lured into theaters with the promise of "The Flying Wedge—cleverest strategy in the history of warfare!"

Let it be. He sits now, on the edge of a hill in Spain, staring at a blood red sunset, reading Herodotus. He is alone, preparing for the next day's shooting. The English contingent of the cast—Ralph Richardson and the others—tend not to mix. The American actors are younger than he is. He sits with a drink, looks up from the book, a little drunk, thinks, grants himself the thought: Not bad. To have come this far, at least. To Spain. From San Francisco. From the war, from a California boyhood. Not bad.

He is caught up, too, in Herodotus. The stories are great. From Herodotus, he learns that the Persians, seizing a Greek boat, chose for sacrifice not the fiercest warrior but the handsomest. That Xerxes, when a storm over the Hellespont destroyed his bridges, had the waters whipped in punishment. And then the best: when a spy came to observe the Spartans, expecting to find, on the eve of their destruction, fear and trembling among the small band, he saw, instead, men combing their long hair, and took such vanity as a sign of weakness.

He looks up when he reads that. The light is about to go entirely, and he has to squint to stare into it. He has a tumbler of bourbon in his hand, and his breathing has changed, gradually. He is startled, though in a quiet way, by what he has just read. All these years, and he has waited to figure out a way to say something other than what's in the lines, how to make the separate compact all the greats knew how to make. And now it comes to him, this late, on a hill in Spain.

Late September, 1962. School days. Baseball in the afternoon has come to seem inappropriate. The grass is like straw now, and Saturdays are for the movies.

Someone knows this. The hunger of pre-adolescent boys

has been prepared for, a steady succession of masculine adventures made ready. Gladiators, foot soldiers, men in prison. Grimace and forearm and sinew. The world presented to boys as an inheritance this second autumn of the Kennedy administration still comes down to a desperate choice, to be made in tight quarters, by a man with a weapon in his hand.

There is something almost numbing about it.

You are twelve now. In the lobby, halfway through this boring movie about the battle of Thermopylae, buying your second bag of popcorn of the day, you look at the light pouring into this theater from outdoors. It occurs to you, briefly, that there might be something else to do, a way to use that light, and your life, other than the ways that seem preordained. It is not, after all, exciting to watch a lot of gladiators smashing swords and flinging arrows at one another. You wait for the moments of blood, the severed arms. But such rewards seem, suddenly, small. You know you are special. You will stand in the light and people will watch you someday. It is, in this instant, a certainty, the high opinion you have always held of yourself, and for a moment you consider dashing out into the afternoon. Running, just running. No purpose or cause. Running in celebration of yourself.

Habit, though, is strong. You accept the popcorn from someone. You push through the lobby doors and go once more into the dark. Suddenly, he is up there. The familiar face. Who pays attention to the gods of the movies? They do this, and they do that. But this is a man your mother loved one summer, three years ago. A lifetime, really. And once, even longer ago, you watched him in a drive-in, when your parents were young and held hands. Now he is making a speech to men who are about to die, men who are combing their hair. The Spartans are supposed to teach us all a lesson: about fighting against odds, about valor, about the unquenchable thirst for freedom. All of that is vague. You *are* free, and don't need to be taught a lesson about it. But here is this man, and it is suddenly uncomfortable to watch him, as if he has put his hand on your shoulder and whispered something in your ear. You take your seat, and try to ignore it.

But afterward, on the sidewalk, you find you cannot quite let go of it. You are waiting for your father to come and pick you up. Other boys are there, too, your friends, but you are apart from them. You father cannot come soon enough, because the afternoon is hot, and because every car that passes contains a man, a tired man, going on a chore, preparing to make a left turn, a man with a list in his head. You are convinced that all of them, your father, too, once felt the very specialness you felt so intently not half an hour ago. It is unbearable to think this, and so you start to run, into that light that seemed so beckoning, that light you thought existed solely so that you could run in it. That feeling has gone away, but you run anyway, away from the thing that Richard Egan whispered in your ear while he said his lines, told his soldiers to be brave, and have valor, though they would die the next day. You are running as though you could outrun your own story.

ABOUT THE AUTHOR

ANTHONY GIARDINA is the author of the novels *Men with Debts* and *A Boy's Pretensions* as well as a number of plays that have been produced in New York at Playwrights Horizons and the Manhattan Theatre Club and regionally at Seattle Rep, Washington's Arena Stage, and Yale Rep. His stories and essays have appeared in *Harper's*, *Esquire*, and *GQ*. He lives in Northampton, Massachusetts, with his wife, Eileen, and their daughters, Nicola and Sophia.

ABOUT THE TYPE

The text of this book was set in Janson, a misnamed typeface designed in about 1690 by Nicholas Kis, a Hungarian in Amsterdam. In 1919 the matrices became the property of the Stempel Foundry in Frankfurt. It is an old-style book face of excellent clarity and sharpness. Janson serifs are concave and splayed; the contrast between thick and thin strokes is marked.

Printed in the United States
by Baker & Taylor Publisher Services